"You're a legend, you know. Whether you believe it or not."

Cahill straightened and said gruffly, "You have to stop looking at me that way, Agent Dunlop. You and I both know it can't happen."

Pru almost gasped. She'd let down her guard for one split second, and he'd seen right through her. He *knew*. "What can't happen?" she tried to bluff.

"You know what I'm talking about." His tone remained stern. "I saw it in your eyes just now. I felt it in the car yesterday. I'll admit, I'm attracted to you, too, but I repeat, it can't happen. It wouldn't do either of our careers any good."

He was attracted to her, too? Since when? *Oh, my God*. Pru fought the smile that tugged at her lips. "I don't know what to say. So…what do…"

"We don't do anything. We ignore this until it goes away."

"Okay, but…what if it doesn't go away?"

He frowned. "It will. It always does."

Maybe for you, Pru thought.

Dear Harlequin Intrigue Reader,

You won't be able to resist a single one of our May books. We have a lineup so shiver inducing that you may forget summer's almost here!

- *Executive Bodyguard* is the second book in Debra Webb's exciting new trilogy, THE ENFORCERS. For the thrilling conclusion, be sure you pick up *Man of Her Dreams* in June.

- Amanda Stevens concludes her MATCHMAKERS UNDERGROUND series with *Matters of Seduction*. And the Montana McCalls are back, in B.J. Daniels's *Ambushed!*

- We also have two special premiers for you. Kathleen Long debuts in Harlequin Intrigue with *Silent Warning*, a chilling thriller. And LIPSTICK LTD., our special promotion featuring sexy, sassy sleuths, kicks off with Darlene Scalera's *Straight Silver*.

- A few of your favorite Harlequin Intrigue authors have some special books you'll love. Rita Herron's *A Breath Away* is available this month from HQN Books. And, in June, Joanna Wayne's *The Gentlemen's Club* is being published by Signature Spotlight.

Harlequin Intrigue brings you the best in breathtaking romantic suspense with six fabulous books to enjoy. Please write to us—we love to hear from our readers.

Sincerely,

Denise O'Sullivan
Senior Editor
Harlequin Intrigue

MATTERS OF SEDUCTION
AMANDA STEVENS

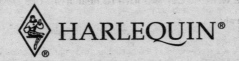

HARLEQUIN®

TORONTO • NEW YORK • LONDON
AMSTERDAM • PARIS • SYDNEY • HAMBURG
STOCKHOLM • ATHENS • TOKYO • MILAN • MADRID
PRAGUE • WARSAW • BUDAPEST • AUCKLAND

ISBN 0-373-22844-9

MATTERS OF SEDUCTION

Copyright © 2005 by Marilyn Medlock Amann

This edition published by arrangement with Harlequin Books S.A.

® and TM are trademarks of the publisher. Trademarks indicated with ® are registered in the United States Patent and Trademark Office, the Canadian Trade Marks Office and in other countries.

www.eHarlequin.com

Printed in U.S.A.

ABOUT THE AUTHOR

The author of over thirty novels, Amanda Stevens is the recipient of Career Achievement awards in both Romantic Mystery and Romantic Suspense from *Romantic Times* magazine. She has been nominated for numerous Reviewers' Choice awards and has been a RITA® Award finalist in the Gothic/Romantic Suspense category. She resides in Houston, Texas.

Books by Amanda Stevens

CAST OF CHARACTERS

Special Agent Prudence Dunlop—Her career is threatened by an elusive killer…and by the one man she can't have.

Special Agent John Cahill—A legend among his colleagues, this G-man has his own demons to battle.

Special Agent Tim Sessions—He's good at what he does. Very, very good.

Sergeant Janet Stryker—How far will this ambitious detective go to get her man?

Sergeant Barry Reed—Is he tired of being upstaged by his flamboyant partner?

Clare McDonald—A woman with a deadly secret.

Tiffany Beaumont—Her friend wasn't the only one with secrets.

John Allen Stiles—A convicted serial killer, his deadly reach extends beyond his jail cell.

Sid Zellman—Stiles's new attorney is a man with his own compulsions.

Greg Oldman—Zellman's handsome and enigmatic assistant.

Naomi Wallis—She seems to have an unnatural attachment to Stiles.

Danny Costello—He was hired to follow Clare McDonald. Can he now identify her killer?

Max Tripp—His P.I. agency promises his rich clients a connection with the woman of their dreams. Could one of his clients be a killer?

Prologue

I don't hate women, okay? Let's make that clear from the start. Quite the contrary, I adore women. I find them endlessly fascinating. I can watch them for hours and never grow bored. They're my canvas, you see. My clay. Even more, they're my air and water. Without them, I would cease to exist.

So, no, I don't hate women, nor do I take their lives for sadistic pleasure. I'm not on a mission. I'm not a thrill seeker. I don't hear voices inside my head. I don't fit any of your profiles because I'm not like any killer you've ever known.

Special Agent John Cahill stopped the tape, rewound, and then pressed Play as he got up from his desk and strode to the window to stare out. A chill ran up his spine as the distorted voice behind him droned on. He couldn't identify the speaker, but there was something disturbingly familiar about the message.

The tape had been included in a stack of reports

and crime scene photos sent to him by Lieutenant Bill Mayberry of the Houston Police Department, along with a request that he review the cases ASAP. The original tape had been delivered to HPD head-quarters, addressed simply to the Homicide Division, the day after the second body had been discovered in the Montrose area of the city.

So far, the beleaguered HPD crime lab had had no luck with voice analysis or in tracing the package back to the sender. The tape was a curiosity, to say the least, but Mayberry had stressed in their initial phone conversation that he had no idea if it was even rele-vant to the cases. His instincts told him that it was, though, and he was worried.

The two recent homicides bore eerie similarities to a killing spree that had occurred in Houston two years ago. The sensationalized case had become known as the Casanova Murders because of the champagne, candles and rose petals found at the crime scenes and the single red rose placed in the victims' hands.

According to Dr. Darian West, a criminal psy-chologist who had been instrumental in solving the case, Casanova—aka John Allen Stiles—had stalked his victims before he raped and strangled them. He had gotten to know them and then they'd willingly let him into their homes because, over the course of days or even weeks, they'd become infatuated with him.

Mayberry's request regarding the two recent hom-icides was simple. He wanted a professional assessment as to whether or not they were looking for the same suspect in both cases.

Left unspoken, of course, was the police lieutenant's real fear. Could HPD have a copycat killer on its hands?

Each time Cahill listened to the tape, the dread inside him deepened. There was something about that voice…

The guy sounded calm and reasonable, which worried Cahill a great deal.

Raving lunatics were the easy ones. It was the quiet, cerebral, Ted-Bundy-boy-next-door types that kept him awake at night.

Jessie, he thought suddenly. She'd planned to visit this weekend, but now he'd have to call and make some excuse about why she couldn't come. If he was going to involve himself in this case, he didn't want her around.

And he was going to get involved. He could feel the adrenaline surging already, as much as he didn't want to admit it. He'd been trying to slowly phase himself out of the unit, and maybe this case could finally be his swan song. He'd known for a while now that it was time to move on. Time to get out of the business of death.

He didn't want the nightmares that followed him home at night to ever touch Jessie again.

And yet, here he was, being sucked back in….

Which was why he'd have to discourage her from

coming this weekend. He was probably overreacting, but he couldn't afford to take that chance. Not with Jessie. She meant too much to him.

She meant everything to him.

He rubbed a hand across his tired eyes. Damn it, they didn't need another setback. Not when they were getting along so well, making real progress in a relationship that had been strained for far too long. Ever since...

No, he wouldn't think about that. It didn't do either of them any good to rehash the past. To dwell on the what-ifs. God knows, he'd nearly driven himself crazy with that game.

Taking a few deep breaths, he struggled to control the blind rage that still threatened to explode in moments of weakness or exhaustion. Slowly, he unclenched his fists as he stared out at the deepening twilight.

Behind him, the tape came to an end, but he didn't bother to restart it. Not yet. Instead, he concentrated on the twinkling lights of the Houston skyline. He'd lived at the same location for over a year now, but he still wasn't used to the view. He couldn't get used to a lot of things. The apartment just didn't seem like home to him. It was a place where he showered and slept, where he had an occasional meal, but it wasn't home.

Home was a four-bedroom ranch in a northwest suburb surrounded by loblolly pines and a well-tended lawn. A driveway littered with bicycles and a backyard swimming pool teeming with noisy adolescents. It was where he retreated to after a long day spent in some very dark places, but that home didn't exist anymore. Except in his memories.

Oh, the house was still there. He'd driven past a few months ago in another moment of weakness. The wood trim had been freshly painted and new landscaping had been put in. He'd felt a pang of something that might have been resentment at how great the place looked.

Which was crazy. He'd never wanted that house in the first place, but his ex-wife had had her heart set on it. After years of scrimping and saving to make the mortgage payments, he should feel nothing now but relief to have that burden lifted from his shoulders. He should be enjoying his life as a single man again. After all, he wasn't over the hill yet. He wasn't even forty, or so he tried to convince himself, but when he counted up, he realized his next birthday loomed just around the corner.

The house was gone, his ex-wife had a new boyfriend and his daughter was finally adjusting to college life at the University of Houston. He didn't have a single worry these days.

Except for that voice on the tape, and the familiar sense of evil lurking around the next corner.

Turning from the window, he picked up the phone to call Jessie, but instead he pressed Play again and closed his eyes as he listened to that voice.

...don't fit any of your profiles because I'm not like any killer you've ever known. I wasn't a bed wetter or a fire starter as a child, and I've never tortured small animals. I wasn't abused, abandoned or even particularly misunderstood. I'm neither a misfit nor the guy next door. I'm gainfully employed, well educated, a real "catch" some might even say.

I kill for one reason and one reason only...because I can.

Chapter One

Tiffany Amber Beaumont was one of those people who could only be taken in small doses, which was why Prudence Dunlop normally went out of her way to avoid the pesky woman. She was self-absorbed, shallow and irritatingly persistent. So persistent, in fact, that when she'd called after work that day, Pru—against her better judgment—had agreed to meet her for drinks.

On the up side, Pru supposed that even Tiffany's company was preferable to spending a rainy Monday night alone in her apartment.

Not that she minded being alone. She'd certainly had enough practice and besides, she'd never been the type who easily bored of her own company. In fact, Pru *liked* being by herself.

Lately, however, all those solitary evenings were giving her a little too much time to think about her work. To wonder about her future. To fantasize about a man who barely even knew she was alive.

"...so you can see why I'm so worried," Tiffany fretted as the waiter placed a fresh apple martini before her.

Momentarily distracted by the guy's dimpled smile, Pru tried to pick up the thread of the conversation. "Not really. Clare is a grown woman, after all."

"A grown woman who is acting like a stranger." Oblivious to the waiter's appreciative glances, Tiffany ignored the poor guy until he finally gave up and left. Pru tracked his retreat with her own appreciative gaze.

"Come on." Tiffany's voice was edged with impatience. "Remember how chatty she used to be in high school? She couldn't wait to tell us every little detail about her boyfriends. She's never been the secretive type, but now, suddenly, she won't tell me anything about this guy. Not his name, where he lives, what he does for a living. *Nada.*" She sipped her drink. "That's just not like her and you know it."

Actually, Pru didn't know any such thing. She hadn't seen Clare McDonald in years because she'd long ago given up on her high school friendships. She'd never had much in common with any of those girls, anyway. The only reason she kept in touch with Tiffany was because their mothers were best friends.

Since childhood, Valerie Dunlop and Theresa Beaumont had been like sisters, and their fondest wish had been for their daughters to become just as close. But Tiffany and Pru were polar opposites.

Pru had to admit, though, that Tiffany had more than held her own since high school. Now a successful advertising executive, she certainly looked and dressed the part.

Pru recognized the pink power suit. It was from a high-end designer, and the leather slingbacks were unmistakably Italian. Pru's mother owned an exclusive uptown boutique and before that, she'd been a buyer for Neiman Marcus. Pru couldn't have been Valerie Dunlop's daughter for twenty-eight years and not picked up *something* of her fashion sense.

Not that you could tell by looking at her, Pru thought dryly. The closest she came to haute couture these days was leafing through the pages of *Vogue* magazine in the hair salon. Even with her mother's generous discount, she couldn't afford to shop at the pricey boutique.

But it didn't matter. She'd long ago accepted the fact that she would never be in Tiffany's and Clare's league, much less her mother's. She'd never be as beautiful or as impossibly skinny as that glamorous trio, but that was okay, too. She was fit and healthy and could run three miles in just under twenty-two minutes. That had to count for something, if she could believe the slow once-over from the guy seated at the end of the bar.

He'd been checking her out ever since he'd arrived a few minutes earlier. He wasn't as cute as the waiter, but he had an interesting face and dark, sultry eyes.

Not as dark as John Cahill's, of course. Nor as sultry. But then, whose were?

Pru let her gaze linger as she considered her options. She could flash the guy a smile and see if he approached their table, or she could go over to the bar and strike up a conversation with him. If something sparked, she could see where it led.

For a split second, she gave her imagination free rein as she fantasized about a night of hot sex in a stranger's bed.

But it wasn't a stranger's dark eyes she imagined staring down at her. It was John Cahill's.

She couldn't seem to get him out of her head, but she had to. For the sake of her career and her own peace of mind, she had to accept the fact that John Cahill was not the man for her.

Banishing his image to the far recesses of her mind, she returned her attention to Tiffany, who was already halfway through her second drink.

Pru toyed with her own glass. "Look, maybe the reason Clare hasn't confided in you yet is because the relationship isn't serious. Did you ever think of that?"

"Since when has that ever stopped her?" Tiffany demanded. "Besides, it's not true. I can tell she's in love just by looking at her. So why won't she let me meet him? Unless…"

"Unless what?" Pru pressed.

"Unless it's his idea. What if he's one of those abusive men who knows how to sweep a woman off her feet, and then tries to isolate her from her friends and family?"

Pru frowned. "Don't you think you're jumping to conclusions? Maybe she's just not ready to talk about him."

"And maybe by the time she is ready, it'll be too late." Tiffany's blue eyes pleaded with her. "Come on, Pru. You have to do something."

"Me?" Pru said in surprise. "This is none of my business. I don't even know why you're telling me about it."

"Because you work for the FBI, for crying out loud! There must be some way you can find out what this guy is up to."

Pru's duties in the Criminal Investigations Division were more analytical than investigative in nature. She'd been stuck behind a computer far longer than she'd planned. It was a sore point, but she didn't feel like explaining all that to Tiffany. "I'm sorry, but I can't help you."

"Why not?" she asked in exasperation. "Can't you at least run a background check or something?"

"No, I can't." Pru decided to be blunt. That was the only way to get through to Tiffany. "Even if I wanted to get involved, which I don't, and even if I could get authorization from my section chief, which I can't, you don't have a name, address or place of employment. You don't have anything. How am I supposed to run a background check on that?"

"You could have him followed," Tiffany said in a rush. "That way, you could find out where he lives and then you could..." She trailed off as Pru began to shake her head. "Oh, okay. I get it. You've already made up your mind so you're not even willing to hear me out. You think I'm overreacting, and maybe I am. But I'm telling you, Pru, something isn't right about this guy. I can feel it."

"Unfortunately, that still isn't a basis for launching a federal investigation."

"How can you say that when you haven't even heard the whole story?" Tiffany persisted.

Pru tried to hide her irritation. "All right, then let me hear the whole story."

Tiffany scowled at her skeptical tone. "Are you going to keep an open mind?"

"I'll try."

"I suppose that'll have to do." Tiffany folded her arms on the table and leaned forward. "I'm not supposed to say anything about this. Clare made me promise not to tell anyone, but under the circumstances..." She bit her lip. "Pru...she thinks someone's following her."

Pru felt a slight chill go up her spine. "What do you mean, following her?"

"Just that," Tiffany said. "Footsteps behind her. The same car following her on the freeway two days in a row."

"Does she know who it is?"

Tiffany's expression clouded. "She's never actually *seen* anyone, but she thinks it might be this creep at work...Sid Zellman."

"Has she gone to the police?"

"No, because there's nothing they can do. Whoever he is, he hasn't threatened her or anything like that. He just...follows her. She won't admit it, but I can tell she's really freaked out about it."

"Then I don't understand," Pru said. "Why wouldn't she want you to tell anyone about it?"

"She doesn't want the partners at her firm to start thinking of her as a liability. And besides, if it is this Sid Zellman person, he seems to have some pretty heavy-duty clout."

"So why are you telling me about it now? Are you suggesting there's some kind of connection between the guy she's seeing and whoever is following her?"

If anyone was following her. It was entirely possible that Clare had imagined the whole thing. Both she and Tiffany had always been a bit melodramatic.

Tiffany tucked a strand of blond hair behind one ear. Diamonds glittered on her lobes, and Pru wondered if they were real. Knowing Tiffany, they were. "All I know is that there have been a lot of odd coincidences lately."

"Such as?"

Tiffany hesitated. "A day or two before Clare told me about someone following her, I had something strange happen to me. I'd stopped in for coffee at a little place across the street from my building, and a guy walked up to me and told me his name was Todd Hollister. He seemed to know me, and then he reminded me that we'd gone to high school together."

"Todd Hollister," Pru murmured, trying to put a face to the name.

"I know. I didn't remember him, either. And it's always so awkward when someone recognizes you and you can't place them to save your life." She paused to shoo away the hopeful waiter. "Anyway, we talked for a few minutes while we finished our coffee, and then he left. I didn't think too much about it until later when I realized that, even though he'd been the one to approach me, I'd done most of the talking."

Imagine that. Pru took a sip of her drink. "What did you talk about?"

"Mundane stuff at first. Do you ever see so-and-so and what's such-and-such up to these days and did what's-her-name ever get married. And then he started asking a lot of questions about Clare. Like I said, I didn't think anything of it at the time because everyone in school knew how close she and I were. It was only natural that he'd ask about her. But, looking back, I'm not so sure his questions were all that casual."

"You think he was pumping you for information about her?"

"Yes. That's exactly what I think."

"What did Clare say when you told her?"

Tiffany glanced away. "That's just it. I didn't tell her because I didn't want to worry her. After a few days, though, when I couldn't stop thinking about this guy, I decided to look him up in our yearbook."

"And?"

"It wasn't him."

"Are you sure? It could have been a bad photograph," Pru suggested. "And people do change in ten years."

"That's what I tried to tell myself. Our bumping into each other didn't mean anything and his questions about Clare were harmless. But now I'm not so sure. Now I'm starting to put all these things together—this guy showing up at the coffeehouse claiming to be someone he's not, Clare being followed, a new boyfriend she won't talk about…" Tiffany gripped the table. "Pru. What if all these things aren't coincidences? What if she really is in some kind of danger?"

Pru paused, choosing her words with care. "Look, I can see you're really worried about this, but I still say you may be jumping to conclusions. And I'm not sure how I can help. Unless you want me to talk to Clare."

Alarm flickered in Tiffany's blue eyes. "No, don't do that. She'd know I put you up to it, and I don't want to upset her. Things have been pretty tense between us lately as it is. Whatever we decide to do, we have to be discreet."

"Whatever *we* decide to do? Tiffany—"

"Don't say it," she begged. "Don't say you won't help me. You have to. I don't have anyone else to turn to."

Pru raked fingers through her brown hair. She'd pinned it up earlier in the day to get it out of her way, but strands were tumbling out of the clasp, making her look as bedraggled and worn-out as she felt tonight. "Look, I'd like to help. I really would. But this isn't a matter for the FBI. There's nothing I can do officially, and without a name or address, there's very little I can do unofficially."

"What if you had a fingerprint?" Tiffany eyed Pru with cagey eagerness. "Couldn't you start from there?"

"You're telling me you have this guy's fingerprint?"

"I have *someone's* fingerprint." Tiffany pawed in her leather tote before uncovering a packet of photographs that she shoved across the table toward Pru. "No, be careful!" she said when Pru started to open the envelope. "Those were taken a few weeks ago at Clare's birthday party. I'd just gotten them back when I went into the coffee shop that day, and Todd Hollister, or whoever that man was, saw me looking at them. I dropped one and he handed it back to me. I'm pretty sure he left fingerprints on it. I noticed because it always drives me crazy when people are careless with photographs. Anyway, I put the pack back in my purse, and it's been there ever since. Isn't it possible his prints could still be on that pic-

ture? Couldn't you lift one of them and run it through
the FBI computers or something?"

Pru had a feeling that had been Tiffany's intent all
along, she'd just taken a roundabout way of getting
there. "What makes you think his fingerprints would
even be in the database?"

Tiffany shrugged. "I don't. But it's worth a shot,
isn't it? If you get a match and they belong to Todd
Hollister, then I'll know he is who he says he is and
our bumping into each other was a coincidence. But
if they belong to someone else…" Her gaze darkened. "Clare could really be in trouble."

CLARE MCDONALD stepped out of the elevator and hurried across the parking garage toward her car. "Of all
the days to have to work late," she grumbled to herself.

An attorney with a prestigious downtown law firm,
she and the other low-level associates were assigned
most of the grunt work while the partners enjoyed all
the glory. That was the way of the world, and Clare
tried to comfort herself with the knowledge that it
wouldn't be like that forever. She was smart, savvy
and extremely ambitious. A girl could go far on those
attributes alone, but throw in a great pair of legs and
nothing could stop her.

Already life was looking up. One of the senior
partners had specifically asked to have her assigned
to his case, which meant that she was making a name
for herself in the firm. The right people were notic-

ing-her, and that put her a notch above most of the competition.

And she had a new man in her life.

Her heart fluttered at the knowledge that they would soon be together, and if everything went according to plan…they would be lovers by midnight.

She couldn't stop smiling at that prospect.

They'd been seeing each other for nearly two weeks but hadn't slept together yet. His idea. She would have tumbled into bed with him on that first night, she'd been that infatuated, but he'd wanted to hold off.

And now Clare readily conceded that he'd been right. The tension that had been building between them was excruciating and thrilling and wonderful, but strangely enough, now that the moment was finally at hand, she felt a bit nervous about it.

What if she didn't please him?

But that was crazy. She'd never had any complaints, had she? Quite the opposite, in fact. No reason to assume that tonight would lead to anything other than explosive, earth-shattering sex.

Her heart started to pound as she imagined that first exquisite moment when their bodies became one….

She squirmed a little in anticipation, but first things first. The stage had to be properly set. Mood was everything, he insisted.

Which meant she had to hurry. She had to go by the florist's for roses and the liquor store for a bottle of champagne. So many things still left to do. She mentally began to prepare a list as she strode toward her car, her high heels clicking against the pavement. Everyone else had gone home hours ago, and now the level she'd parked on that morning was almost deserted.

Shifting her briefcase to her left hand, she dug in her shoulder bag for her keys. When she couldn't find them, she cursed softly and set the case on the concrete floor while she rifled through her purse.

Keys finally in hand, she stooped to retrieve her briefcase. And that's when she heard the footsteps. Slow and methodical, like a hunter stalking his prey.

Gooseflesh prickled along her spine as she whirled.

The footsteps stopped.

She couldn't see anyone, but that didn't mean he wasn't there. The lighting was dim in the garage, and the concrete support beams could easily provide a hiding place.

"Hello," she called in a tremulous voice. "Anyone there?"

No one answered, of course. He never did. He never said anything to her. Never showed himself. But she knew he was there, just the same. Following her, watching her.

Her hand slid inside her purse and fastened around the smooth cylinder of Mace. She thumbed off the top and held the can in front of her.

"Who's there?" she called again.

Still no answer, but after a moment, she heard his footsteps again, this time walking away from her. Frantically, she scanned the garage and saw only a fleeting shadow near the stairwell.

For one desperate moment, Clare considered chasing him down and finding out once and for all the identity of her tormentor.

But it was only a passing whim. In the next instant, she spun and rushed to her car. Using the remote to unlock her door, she climbed inside and then locked herself in. With shaking fingers, she started the ignition, and only when she emerged into the steady flow of traffic on Main Street did she begin to relax.

The footsteps had probably been nothing more than her imagination, she tried to tell herself. The shadow near the stairwell nothing more than…a shadow.

After all, a stalker usually made contact, didn't he? Wrote letters, made obscene or threatening phone calls. *Something.* She hadn't caught so much as a glimpse of anyone following her, and yet she couldn't shake the notion at times that she was being watched.

And she *had* heard footsteps, damn it.

What if it really was Sid Zellman?

She shuddered as an image of the creepy man materialized in her head. He'd been at the firm forever, but no one seemed to know much about him. There were rumors, of course, but the details were always a little sketchy.

He never appeared in court. Clare knew that much. Jared Hathaway, another partner, handled all the litigation for him. He even met with Zellman's clients. It was a strange setup, but Clare didn't question it. She didn't want the partners to think she was the gossipy type and besides, all she wanted to do was keep her distance from Zellman. Once when she'd run into him in the hallway, he'd stared at her in such a way as to make her think he might not be playing with a full deck. After that, Clare tried to avoid him.

And now she tried to put him out of her mind. She had much more important things to think about at the moment. The evening stretched before her and she smiled again in anticipation. *Tonight....*

Finishing her errands, she arrived home forty-five minutes later and quickly jumped into the shower. A relaxing bath would have been nice, but she didn't have time for that. Maybe later they could bathe together...

Quickly putting the finishing touches to her make-up, she rose from her dressing table and slithered into the black jersey dress she'd laid on the bed. It had the texture and fit of fine lingerie, and she slid her hands down her sides, luxuriating in the erotic feel. Next, she slipped into the four-inch stiletto heels—a little gift to herself to help celebrate what she had come to think of as The Night.

She was probably making too much of it, she cautioned herself, as she spritzed the air with her favorite perfume, then waltzed through the scent. This was hardly her first time, after all. At twenty-eight, she'd had plenty of lovers, but she couldn't remember the last time she'd been so thoroughly swept off her feet.

They'd been slow-dancing to this point for days now, but every step, every move, every dip and swirl had been carefully choreographed for her maximum pleasure, he'd promised.

She shivered now as she imagined all the ways his hard body could pleasure her. Forget seduction. She wanted him *now*….

"Patience," he'd whispered when she'd begged him to make love to her last night. And then his tongue had traced her lips before plunging inside her mouth.

God, but he knew how to use that tongue. Within a matter of moments, he'd had her moaning and writhing uncontrollably as she pulled him on top of her and slid her hand down, down, down until she touched him…

Her legs went weak with excitement as she remembered the way he swelled against her hand, the way he touched her in return…

Pressing her palm against her chest, she felt the pounding rhythm of her heart. "Patience," she whispered on a quivering breath.

Taking one final check of her appearance, she hurried downstairs and poured a glass of wine to settle her nerves.

Cradling the delicate stem between her fingers, she glanced around. The place looked fantastic, if she did say so herself. Candles flickered from an ornate candelabrum on the dining room table; in the living room, a bottle of champagne chilled in a silver bucket. She'd set out her grandmother's crystal flutes, and the effect was understated elegance complemented by a background of romantic music. As her gaze followed the trail of scarlet rose petals up the stairs, she sighed in satisfaction.

Perfect. Everything was just the way he wanted it. He would be so pleased with her attention to detail.

She frowned as she lifted the glass to her lips. Everything was ready. *She* was ready. So why that shiver of unease up her spine?

Why those worrisome little doubts that maybe, just maybe, he was too good to be true?

He wasn't at all the sort of man she was normally attracted to. In fact, he was the kind of guy she might easily have overlooked if not for a chance encounter in an elevator.

But he knew how to treat her. He knew what she wanted and when and how she wanted it. He seemed to intuit her every need, her every desire, and his eyes—just before he kissed her—mirrored her deepest, darkest fantasies.

When he looked at her that way, she could forget her doubts. She could easily ignore that nagging premonition that something wasn't quite right about him.

The doorbell rang, and in her nervousness, she spilled a little wine down the front of her dress. She didn't really care. With any luck, she'd be out of her clothes before he even noticed.

Rushing to let him in, she caught a glimpse of the rose petals out of the corner of her eye, and for just a split second, the splash of crimson spilling down the stairs reminded her of blood.

She nudged the image away and, plastering a seductive smile on her face, opened the door to her would-be lover.

Chapter Two

Once a bohemian enclave for artists and musicians, the Montrose area of Houston had slowly been evolving over the past twenty years. The free spirit was alive and well, but progress had brought money to the galleries, boutiques and trendy eateries that lined the eclectic streets.

The true starving artists had moved to the wards closer to downtown, and now the quaint cottages and bungalows were being overshadowed by a glut of apartments and condos.

Cahill knew the area. He'd grown up in Houston, but he'd spent the first decade of his career in Washington before a rash of serial murders in Southeast Texas had brought him back here to establish a local arm of SKURRT—Serial Killer Unit Rapid Response Team.

The moment he turned onto Willard, he spotted the squad cars and the Crime Scene Unit van that were parked at the curb in front of a row of town houses.

The inevitable crowd of onlookers had already gathered on the sidewalk. A few of the more aggressively curious pressed against the police cars and shouted questions to the officers manning the yellow-ribboned perimeter, but most of the neighbors kept their distance. They huddled in small groups beneath the catalpa trees or stood alone in their doorways as they watched with a mixture of excitement and fear.

Crime was hardly a stranger in Montrose. The area had more than its share of robberies, domestic disputes and even homicides, but the violence was usually confined to the less sophisticated fringes. The town houses and renovated bungalows were supposed to be a haven for the young, hip professionals who either had no desire to live in or couldn't afford the more conservative and pricey neighborhoods of West University and Memorial.

So the lawyers, technical consultants and midlevel executives hung back, not wanting to get involved. Not wanting to sully a pleasant morning with the messy reality of murder.

Cahill pulled to the curb behind the Crime Scene Unit and got out. It was late September, but the steamy humidity of a Gulf-coast Indian summer enveloped him like the cloying heat of a South American jungle. There were no orchids here, however. No exotic birds twittering in the treetops as he walked down the street. Just the murmur of voices mingling with the distant spit of a water sprinkler.

He stepped over the crime scene tape and flashed his credentials to the two officers guarding the perimeter. They gave him a curious glance before waving him through, and Cahill headed up a walkway lined with terra-cotta pots of purple bougainvillea and, in the shady areas, African impatiens.

As he approached the front door, he noted the telltale residue of fingerprint powder that still clung to the bronze knocker where the metal had been dusted for latents.

He stood on the stoop, hesitant, for some reason he didn't understand, to turn the knob and walk inside.

Or maybe he did understand. After fifteen years of chasing monsters, maybe he'd finally had enough. But the apathy wasn't new. It had been building since Jessie's attack.

Seeing her in the hospital, so wounded and frightened, had shifted the battlefield for Cahill, and he had found himself confronting a whole new army of monsters—guilt, rage, helplessness. And the knowledge that, for all his skill and training, he hadn't been able to keep his own daughter safe.

But the other monsters—the sadistic predators who hunted the innocent—refused to give him a reprieve. They kept crawling out of the sewers, drawing him back into the fight, and as Cahill placed his hand on the doorknob, he felt the familiar dread that clutched like a fist around his heart.

Glancing over his shoulder, he scanned the quiet

street beyond the small group of spectators gathered near the patrol cars. His attention briefly caught on a man standing on the sidewalk across the street. He carried a newspaper under one arm and a brown paper bag in the opposite hand.

His features were hidden behind aviator-style sunglasses and the bill of a baseball cap, and his head was turned in such a way that Cahill had only a brief glimpse of his profile. Cahill didn't recognize him, and yet in that one brief moment, he had the uncanny notion that he knew the man.

...I don't fit any of your profiles because I'm not like any killer you've ever known.

The voice on the tape whispered through Cahill's head so clearly that for a moment, it almost seemed as if he were connecting with the man telepathically.

The man put his fingers to his mouth and whistled. A small, brown terrier shot out of a nearby alley and dashed toward him, leaping and barking excitedly at the bag in the man's hand.

He reached down and patted the dog's head as he clipped a leash to his collar. Then the two of them strolled away.

Cahill watched until they were out of sight, then he turned and stepped inside the town house.

THE FIRST THING he noticed was the chill. The thermostat had been set so low that he found himself shivering as he gazed around. Two patrolmen stood at the bottom of the stairs chatting quietly with one another, and from somewhere nearby—the kitchen, he presumed—he could hear the muffled sound of sobbing.

The town house had an open, airy layout and a cool modern decor in beige and steel-blue. Silk draperies covered the windows, and a crystal chandelier hung over a mahogany dining table that had been set for two.

The place was tidy except for the candle wax that had dripped onto the table and the trail of wilted rose petals that led upstairs.

Cahill's gaze moved from a champagne bucket in the living room to the burned-out candles on the table to the rose petals littering the stairs. The seductive "props" were identical to the photos Lieutenant Mayberry had sent him a few days ago.

The rumble of voices drew him upstairs and, avoiding the petals, he paused once again on the landing to glance around. A set of double doors stood open at the end of the hallway, and from inside came the brisk, professional tone of a CSU investigator as he narrated the setting.

Cahill started down the hallway, his gaze moving over the walls, floor, even the ceiling. The trail of rose petals led straight back to the bedroom, but nothing else seemed out of place except for a faint, exotic scent he couldn't quite place.

Inside the bedroom, two people—homicide detectives, he assumed—stood at the end of the bed, their gazes locked as one on something Cahill couldn't yet see.

The woman, a slender brunette dressed in a navy blazer and snug-fitting jeans, spotted him first, and a frown flicked across her brow before she shifted her focus back to the bed. She looked to be in her mid to late thirties, well-dressed, well-groomed, extremely attractive. And she had attitude.

She said nothing to her companion to alert him of Cahill's presence. It was almost as if by ignoring him, she could pretend he wasn't there.

"Special Agent Cahill? Sorry I'm late."

He turned to see Bill Mayberry trudging up the stairs. He was a tall, muscular man dressed in a suit that looked far too heavy for the sticky weather outside, and in spite of the meat-locker temperature inside, sweat glistened along the police lieutenant's receding hairline.

Cahill knew Mayberry slightly. They'd worked together a few years back on the infamous Boxcar Murders, and his impression of the man was of a hardworking, dedicated cop, seemingly without the ego that sometimes made dealing with local law enforcement personnel a nightmare for federal agents.

"No problem. I just got here myself." Cahill glanced toward the bedroom. "You've got another one, I take it."

Mayberry nodded, his lined face registering the inevitable weariness of a long career in law enforcement. "It's the same deal. Right down to the rose. That's why I asked you to meet me here."

"Okay," Cahill said. "Let's have a look."

As they stepped through the bedroom door, the two detectives finally peeled their gazes from the bed and glanced up.

Mayberry waited for the CSU investigator to finish videotaping the crime scene, then he made the introductions. "Sgt. Janet Stryker, Sgt. Barry Reed, both Homicide. They caught the first case, and I've put them on this one because they're familiar with the particulars. This is Special Agent John Cahill with the FBI. He heads up a team in SKURRT that specializes in this kind of thing."

"SKURRT." Janet Stryker gave him a cool assessment. "Serial Killer Unit Rapid Response Team, right?"

He nodded. "That's right."

"You're a profiler." The contempt in her voice punctuated the resentment flickering in her eyes.

So here was the ego, Cahill thought. And not testosterone-fueled as he might have imagined. "I'm not a profiler. I'm an investigator. I beat the bushes just like you do."

Her lip curled in what might have been a sneer before she returned her attention to the bed.

Mayberry had preceded Cahill into the room, and now he stepped aside to allow Cahill an unimpeded view of the dead woman.

The covers had been stripped away, and she lay on top of a pink satin sheet, her pale, nude body positioned in a funeral pose—legs together and straight out, arms folded over her breasts, hands on top of one another.

A long-stemmed rose had been slipped between her cold fingers, and there were ligature marks on her wrists and ankles. A wider welt encircled her neck.

Her eyes were open, and her long, blond hair was spread so artfully against the pillow that Cahill suspected it had been arranged. She wore makeup—eye shadow, blush, and a deep red lipstick that seemed garish, almost grotesque, against her pale skin.

She wouldn't have been easily subdued. She was slim, but Cahill could see the hard definition of muscle along her forearms and calves. If she'd known what was coming, she would have fought back, but he couldn't detect any defense wounds. Her nails were unbroken, and her pallid skin appeared flawless except for the ligature marks and the faint abdominal discoloration of decomposition.

Her clothing—dress, panties, bra—had been discarded on the floor near the bed, but she still wore her high heels. Candles had been arranged all around the room, and like the tapers in the dining room, they'd burned themselves out.

By all indications, she'd been a willing participant. She might even have agreed to the bondage, but by the time she realized it was getting out of hand, it had been too late.

Mayberry muttered an oath. "Do we know who she is?"

"Clare McDonald," Sgt. Reed supplied. "She was an attorney with Linney, Gardner and Braddock. Their offices are in the Texas National Bank Building downtown. Twenty-eight years old, single, lives alone."

"Who found her?"

"A friend...Tiffany Beaumont." Reed was younger than his partner, probably just under thirty, with a boyish face and a nervous demeanor. He kept running his hand up and down his tie. "She came over this morning and persuaded the property manager to let her in. According to Beaumont, she tried to reach McDonald at work yesterday and was told she'd been out for two days without calling in. That wasn't like her, so Beaumont got worried and started trying to reach her. She left messages on the machine and with McDonald's voice mail, but McDonald never called her back. When Beaumont got home from a business meeting last night, she started calling again. By morning, she'd worked herself up into a panic, so she hightailed it over here and got the property manager to let her in."

"Has she been interviewed?"

Sgt. Reed rubbed the corner of his mouth with his forefinger. He seemed to have a lot of nervous mannerisms. "I spoke with her for a few minutes. She was incoherent, for the most part. We've got someone with her now trying to calm her down."

Cahill studied the body and the crime scene, careful not to let his feelings show on his face. Wouldn't do to let them see how disturbed he was by what he saw. He'd witnessed worse, of course. Much worse. Victims who no longer resembled human beings. Relatively speaking, Clare McDonald had been lucky. She didn't appear to have been tortured before she died, but Cahill was still deeply affected. It might have been Jessie lying there.

"So what do you think?" Mayberry asked him. "Same guy?"

"Could be," he murmured.

"*Could* be?" Something glinted in Janet Stryker's eyes that Cahill didn't like. She seemed a little too excited by the prospect of a sensational case, and he thought he knew why. The publicity could do a lot for an ambitious detective's career, put her on the map, especially if she cultivated a relationship with the media. And Stryker's gender would certainly work in her favor—a female cop tracking a serial killer.

As if reading his mind, she gave Cahill a contemptuous look. "It has to be the same guy. The setup is identical. Candles, champagne, rose petals leading to the body. That can't be a coincidence. Obviously, he fancies himself another Casanova." Her voice turned slightly mocking. "Of course, I'm not the expert here. So why don't you tell us, Agent Cahill? Are we dealing with a copycat or what?"

Cahill ignored her scathing tone and took a moment to gather his thoughts. "As you say, certain aspects of the crime scene are identical to Casanova's, but with one glaring exception. Casanova raped his victims before he strangled them. I've looked over the files you sent me, Lieutenant. There's no evidence that the other two victims—Ellie Markham and Tina Kerr—were sexually assaulted. We won't know until after the autopsy, but I'm willing to bet you're not going to find evidence of penetration here, either. Unlike Casanova, this guy may not be a lust-motivated type of killer. He may. not be killing for sexual gratification."

Janet Stryker lifted a perfectly arched brow. "Oh, no? Then why *does* he kill?"

"That's the intriguing part. A copycat may adopt another killer's *modus operandi,* even his staging and signature, but make no mistake. He has his own compulsions. His own need to kill. He may be drawn to emulate the other killer for a number of reasons, but ultimately, it's because it somehow plays into his own fantasy. But this guy…" Cahill paused, frowning. "He could be something completely different. What we call a surrogate."

Stryker glanced up. "Meaning?"

"He's not succumbing to his own compulsions. He's killing to satisfy someone else's."

"You've got to be kidding me, right?" Stryker moved up beside him, and as she bent over the body, Cahill could smell her perfume. The scent was heavy and intense. Not particularly appealing, he decided. "If he kills, as you say, to satisfy someone else's compulsions, what's in it for him?"

"Acceptance. Praise." Cahill shrugged. "Why do seemingly nice, ordinary women marry death row inmates? They get something from that relationship the rest of us can't understand."

"And because they have a screw loose somewhere," Barry Reed offered from the foot of the bed. He was still rubbing fiercely at the corner of his mouth.

"That, too." Cahill glanced at Mayberry. "Has anyone spoken to John Allen Stiles since these killings started?"

Stryker turned, her eyes cold, sharp, almost accusing. "You're not suggesting Stiles is somehow orchestrating these murders from a maximum security prison, are you?"

"It wouldn't be the first time. There's a thriving subculture created around inmates. The amount of contact they have with the outside world would shock most people. We need to find out if Stiles has had any visitors lately. If he has access to the Internet."

Mayberry ran a hand through his thinning hair. "Look, if you're right about this, the press will bury us in a PR nightmare as soon as they start sniffing around. We need to try and keep a lid on this thing until we figure out what we're dealing with here."

Cahill nodded. "I agree. The less publicity you give this guy, the better."

Mayberry turned to the detectives. "I want you two working this case full-time. I'll get you some help, but I want every lead chased down, I don't care how slim it seems. Make sure you cross every T and dot every I, you got me? You're going to have to bust your asses on this one. I'm also making a formal request for assistance from SKURRT. They'll be able to facilitate anything we need from VICAP and NCIC, as well as offer investigative support," he said, referring to the FBI's Violent Crime and Apprehension Program and the National Crime Information Center. His expression grew even sterner. "I expect Agent Cahill's team to have your full cooperation, understood?"

Reed nodded, but Stryker merely gave Cahill a dismissive glance before turning back to the body. He wondered if she ever got tired of carrying that chip around on her shoulder.

"Another thing. This goes for all of us," Mayberry continued, but Cahill had a feeling he was mainly addressing Stryker. "No interviews, under any circumstances. Keep your mouths shut and your egos under control. We can't afford to let this get away from us. The last thing we need is a full-blown panic on our hands."

It has been said that murder is the perfect seduction.

I believe that to be true, but far be it from me to offer a sociological analysis of why others take lives.

I can only speak for myself in that regard, and as I've stated previously, I don't fit any of your profiles. I'm not like any killer you've ever known. I do, however, offer an intriguing observation: The more society turns serial murder into an object of fascination, the more seductive the act becomes.

In other words, the more attention you give us, the more we want to kill.

Think about that while you hunt me.

In a very real sense, you're searching for a monster of your own creation.

Chapter Three

One week later...

The elevator doors opened and Pru found herself staring up into the darkest eyes she'd ever seen. Not black, as she'd previously thought, but a rich, deep chocolate fringed with jet lashes.

And they were intense. *Man,* were those eyes intense.

He nodded briefly as he stepped onto the elevator and then turned to face forward. The doors slid closed and as the elevator engaged with a slight jerk, Pru's heart fluttered, not because of their ascent, but because of John Cahill's nearness.

After all this time, she couldn't believe she was still so intimidated by him. She'd first met him five years ago in a criminal investigative analysis course he taught at the academy and, like all other students in that class, Pru had been fascinated and more than a little awestruck. Cahill had been aloof, intense and, in spite of his youthful appearance, had already spent ten years on the front lines, tracking and apprehending some of the most violent criminals in the country.

Pru had been drawn to him immediately, but to Cahill, she was only one of dozens of fresh-faced, eager agent trainees who'd hung on his every word. He hadn't given her the time of day back then and, truth be told, Pru would probably have lost a great deal of respect for him if he had. For one thing, the FBI frowned on such fraternization; even more important, he'd been married at the time. Pru had never had much use for husbands who strayed, and she certainly wouldn't have risked her career for one.

But John Cahill wasn't married anymore.

Unfortunately, he still didn't seem inclined to give Pru the time of day.

Running into him so unexpectedly shouldn't fluster her like this, she chided herself. After all, in the six months since her transfer to the Houston field office, she'd seen him plenty of times in the hallway and at meetings. She should be used to those encounters by now.

But she'd never been alone with him, she realized.

Tiny thrills shot up and down her spine as she leaned against the wall, fixated on his back. She couldn't seem to tear her gaze away, but it was a very nice back, so who could blame her?

He wasn't as tall as she remembered him from five years ago, but he was tall enough. Probably around six feet with a lean, muscular body hidden beneath his dark suit.

Luckily, she didn't have to speculate about that muscular body because she'd seen it for herself one day when she'd gone to the gym to let off a little steam. Cahill had been there, attacking his own workout with the ferocity of a man facing a mortal enemy, and Pru had been so distracted by all those glistening muscles that she darn near fell off the treadmill. For the rest of the session, she'd tried to keep her eyes averted from Cahill for fear that someone would pick up on her secret admiration.

But surely she wasn't the only female agent who'd noticed how attractive he was, she thought as she finally tore her gaze from his back. Thick, dark hair. Dreamy eyes. A mouth that looked extremely kissable. What was not to admire?

She forced herself to take a deep breath. Okay, enough. She wasn't a dewy-eyed student anymore; she was a five-year veteran of the Bureau. A twenty-eight-year-old special agent who was dedicated to her career. She had goals and ambition, and she wasn't about to screw up everything she'd worked so hard for over some stupid infatuation. Because, like it or not, John Cahill was every bit as off-limits to her now as he had been at the academy.

Pru had her sights set on SKURRT, and her desire

to become a member of the elite unit had nothing to do with her feelings for John Cahill. In fact, if anything, this dopey crush could hamper her chances if she wasn't careful.

The highly specialized unit in Quantico had seemed out of her reach, but the SKURRT in Houston presented an intriguing possibility. Not only was the Bayou City her hometown, Pru figured she'd have a better shot of making a name for herself on a smaller playing field.

Focusing on her career goals helped steady her resolve, and she drew another deep breath. A golden opportunity had presented itself to her, and she'd be a fool not to take advantage of it.

"Sir?" she blurted before she lost her nerve. "May I have a word with you?"

Cahill turned in surprise, his gaze dropping to her security badge.

Of course, he didn't remember her. No reason why he should.

"Prudence Dunlop," she supplied. "I transferred from Quantico a few months ago."

His dark gaze narrowed a bit. "You're Charlie Dunlop's daughter."

"Yes, sir." Pru tried not to wince. She loved her father and was proud of his thirty-year tenure with the Bureau. But she didn't want to be known as Charlie Dunlop's daughter, which was why she'd waited until his retirement before putting in for a transfer to Houston.

Her father had spent a good portion of his career at the Houston field office, and in this very building was where Pru's own passion for crime fighting had been ignited. Even as a kid, she'd been drawn to her father's profession. While most teenage girls would have killed to have her mother's contacts in the fashion industry, the men—and women—in black had been Pru's idols.

"So how's retirement treating him?" Cahill's tone was friendly, but Pru could tell he was distracted. He was a busy man. It wasn't going to be easy to get his undivided attention. "Getting a lot of fishing in?"

"Not as much as he'd like. He's remodeling a house in Bellaire, and that takes up most of his time. He's becoming quite the carpenter."

"You don't say. Doesn't sound like the Charlie Dunlop I remember."

"Well, you know, he likes to keep busy," Pru said with a shrug. But enough about her dad. She wanted to talk about her future.

"You said you wanted to speak with me. What's on your mind?" Cahill prompted.

Pru beat back her nerves and tried to project a confident demeanor. "I'd like to be considered for SKURRT." Before he could shoot her down, she rushed on. "I've already submitted my request for reassignment. I was hoping you'd had a chance to look it over."

His expression remained noncommittal. "We've been pretty swamped lately. Plus, it takes time for those things to move through the chain of command. I don't have the final word."

"No, but everyone knows your recommendation carries a lot of weight." Then, realizing that might sound too presumptuous, Pru said, "I think you'll see from my application that my qualifications are—"

"Impressive," he cut in. "Undergraduate degree in Criminal Justice from Sam Houston State, master's in Clinical Psychology from University of Houston, finished in the top two percent of your class at the academy, five years in the Criminal Investigations Division, the last three as an analyst in Violent Crime and Major Offenders. And your evaluations are nothing short of glowing. Did I miss anything, Agent Dunlop?"

Pru was stunned by his recitation of her credentials. So he had read her application. He did know who she was. "Uh, no, sir. I believe that covers it."

"I've seen nothing in your file to indicate you're anything other than an excellent special agent. Exactly the kind of person we're looking for in SKURRT. Under normal circumstances, you'd be a strong candidate."

Pru's heart thudded against her chest. Under normal circumstances? What did that mean?

"Unfortunately, I don't see how I can recommend you at this time."

Oh, God, Pru thought. Had her feelings for him been that transparent?

Heat rushed to her face. She tried to swallow past her embarrassment and disappointment.

"It's nothing personal," he added.

Nothing personal?

"HPD is investigating a string of murders in the Montrose area that's beginning to look like a serial. They've asked for our assistance, and the agent we add to the team will spend a lot of time working with me on that case. The problem is…you appear to have a conflict of interest, Agent Dunlop. You knew one of the victims. She was a friend of yours."

Pru frowned. "If you're talking about the third victim, Clare McDonald, we went to high school together, but I saw her only a handful of times over the past ten years."

Still, she'd known Clare well enough to attend her funeral, even though it had been difficult to face Tiffany's accusing eyes. But Pru wasn't the type to beat herself up over something beyond her control. She couldn't have prevented Clare's death. Even if she'd had the authority to launch a full-scale investigation, there wouldn't have been time. According to the medical examiner's best guess, Clare had been murdered only a few hours after Pru had met Tiffany for drinks.

"Sir, I can assure you, I don't have an emotional involvement in this case. At least, not one that would keep me from doing my job objectively."

"But you are involved," Cahill insisted. "From what I understand, you've been in touch with HPD on a number of occasions, pressuring them for information."

"I can explain that." Pru knew she was treading on shaky ground, but she needed to get everything out in the open. Be as honest and forthright as she could and let the chips fall where they would.

The elevator pinged and jolted to a stop. When the doors slid apart, Cahill's arm shot out to hold them open as he glanced at his watch. "I have a meeting at four. If you want to follow me back to my office, I can give you ten minutes."

"Thank you, sir."

He stood aside while Pru exited the elevator and then he stepped off behind her. As they strode toward his office, Pru glanced at the rows of cubicles on either side of the hallway. Behind the partitions, diligent special agent/analysts worked on a constant stream of data being fed into and received from computers all over the world. The information age had changed the face of law enforcement, and people like Pru, who rarely left their desks, were now the norm rather than the exception.

And if she wasn't careful, she could be stuck behind that desk for the rest of her career. Pru shuddered at the prospect.

INSIDE HIS OFFICE, Cahill took a seat behind his desk and motioned Pru to a chair across from him. The phone rang, and as he snatched it up, he indicated that she should wait.

Pru sat with knees together, hands folded neatly on

her lap and tried not to think about those precious ten minutes that were rapidly ticking away. A chance like this didn't come along every day, and she felt an unreasonable irritation toward the person on the other end of the line.

As he listened, Cahill swiveled toward the window, giving Pru an interesting view of his profile. The temptation to stare was too great, so instead she used the opportunity to familiarize herself with his office.

The space was like almost every other office in the building, and Cahill had done very little to personalize it. A single window looked out on the 610 Loop, which would be heavily congested this time of day. A picture of the director hung on the wall behind his desk and a United States flag occupied a corner opposite the window.

Okay, so much for his office.

In spite of her resolve, Pru refocused her attention on Cahill.

He's too old for you, she could almost hear her mother scold her.

Since when does age matter? Dad's nearly fifteen years older than you.

And look how that turned out.

Pru sighed. Her parents had been divorced for just over a year, and even though she'd been in Washington and Virginia for the past five years, she couldn't get used to their living apart. They'd even sold the family home while she'd been away, and her mother had moved into a new condo just south of the Villages, off Voss, while her father had bought his small fixer-upper in Bellaire. Now that he was retired from the Bureau, he spent a good portion of his time at Home Depot.

Pru knew that John Cahill was divorced, too, and he had a grown daughter. Broken marriages were certainly not unusual in their line of work, but her parents had split up after her father retired. Too much togetherness, her mother had explained with a shrug. She'd gotten used to an absentee husband and suddenly having him underfoot drove her crazy.

Pru's father hadn't fought the divorce, but she knew the breakup had hurt him. He still seemed a bit bewildered by it.

She wondered suddenly why Cahill and his wife had split up.

Pru knew very little about the man's personal life. Professionally, however, he was something of a legend in the Houston field office, having been instrumental in solving a number of high-profile cases.

"Agent Dunlop?"

Pru jumped when he said her name. She'd been so lost in thought that she hadn't realized he'd ended his call, and now he'd caught her staring at him.

Embarrassed, Pru glanced away.

"Sorry for the interruption," he said.

"That's fine." Pru hesitated, not certain if she should jump right in with her explanation or wait for his cue.

He propped his arms on his desk and leaned forward. "You were saying?"

She nodded and cleared her throat. "I first contacted the police because I had certain information, mostly thirdhand, that I thought might be relevant to the investigation. I had no idea then that they were requesting FBI assistance."

"Go on."

"As I said, Clare McDonald and I weren't close. I saw her maybe half a dozen times in the past ten years. But we did have a mutual friend…a woman named Tiffany Beaumont."

"She's the one who found the body," Cahill said.

Pru nodded. "She and Clare had been best friends since high school. I mention this because I want to put my interaction with the police in the proper context."

He said nothing.

Pru took a breath. "Just hours before Clare was murdered, Tiffany called and asked me to meet her. She was agitated and wanted to talk about Clare. Evidently, Clare was seeing someone new, and she'd refused to tell Tiffany anything about him—his name, address, place of employment. Clare's behavior was unusual, so Tiffany became convinced this mystery man was trying to isolate her from her friends. She also said that Clare thought she was being followed."

"You relayed this information to the police. It's in the report."

"I know. And I apologize for being redundant, but if you can bear with me, I am leading up to something."

He motioned with his hand for her to proceed.

"Clare didn't know who might be following her, but she suspected someone from work...a man named Sid Zellman. She never actually saw him, though. According to Tiffany, it was more or less a feeling that Clare had."

Cahill glanced at his watch, but when he remained seated, Pru took it to mean she should continue.

"A few days before Tiffany called me, she said a man approached her in a coffee shop claiming to be an old classmate. He said his name was Todd Hollister, and he asked a lot of leading questions about Clare. Tiffany became convinced he wasn't on the up and up, and that's when she called me. She had his thumbprint on a photograph, and she wanted me to run it through the computer. Which I did."

Cahill's gaze sharpened. "You got a match?"

She nodded. "The print belonged to Danny Costello, an ex-cop who now works for a private detective firm run by a former HPD detective named Max Tripp. Tripp's firm caters to rich executives and entrepreneurs who, according to the agency's Web site, are looking for the 'woman of their dreams.'"

"The woman of their dreams," Cahill muttered.

"From what I can tell, this is how the outfit operates. The client comes into the agency with a specific woman in mind, almost always someone that would normally be out his reach. For a substantial fee, Tripp or one of his detectives will conduct a thorough investigation of the woman, including surveillance. By talking to her friends, family, business associates, they find out everything there is to know about her…favorite restaurants, hobbies, where she likes to shop, you name it. Then they design a 'coincidental' meeting with the woman at one of these places."

"And the client is able to connect with her by using the information the investigators feed him," Cahill said.

"That's the objective, yes. It's all handled very discreetly. The woman never knows she's being manipulated."

Cahill sat back in his chair. "And you think someone hired this firm to investigate Clare McDonald? Someone saw her as the woman of his dreams?"

"It fits," Pru said. "She was being followed, and then a P.I. claiming to be an old schoolmate shows up to pump her best friend for information about her."

"Agent Dunlop, are you suggesting this agency is somehow connected to Clare McDonald's murder?"

"I don't now," Pru said with a shrug. "But I think it's worth checking out."

"It's an interesting angle, I'll give you that." Cahill glanced at his watch again, but he still made no move to leave. "Be even more interesting to find out if this agency is connected to either Ellie Markham or Tina Kerr," he said, referring to the other two victims.

"I agree," Pru said. "What I can't understand is why the police haven't already pressured Max Tripp to release his client's name. I can't get HPD to give me a straight answer."

Cahill frowned. "Who are you talking to?"

"A detective named Stryker. Janet Stryker. Do you know her?"

Cahill's expression remained neutral, but Pru saw something flash in his eyes. She wondered what it meant. "I've met her. Did she give you any reason why they haven't pursued the lead?"

"Not really." Pru hesitated. "But I have my own theory."

"You think she's covering for either Costello or Tripp?"

"It wouldn't surprise me. Cops protect their own. Even ex-cops. And let's just say…she wasn't too thrilled when she found out I was a federal agent."

Cahill shrugged. "Put yourself in her place. She's an ambitious detective who's just caught a big case. It wouldn't do her career any good to have the FBI come in and steal her thunder."

Pru thought he was being a little too generous. Janet Stryker might very well be ambitious, but she was also arrogant, manipulative and dismissive. Pru had not found her attitude to be the least bit helpful.

Cahill got up and came around to perch on the edge of his desk. His jacket was unbuttoned and his shirt a bit rumpled after an already long day. He still looked good, though. Too good. Pru found herself wishing he wasn't quite so attractive.

She'd never particularly had a thing for older men, nor did she have a penchant for the forbidden. The simple truth was, John Cahill had fascinated her five years ago, and he fascinated her still.

He was as aloof and intense as ever, but the ensuing years had stolen the remainder of his youth. He had lines around his mouth and eyes and a grim set to his features that she didn't remember from before. Apparently, a lot had happened in those five years, and not much of it good.

"What I'm about to tell you isn't common knowledge, so I'm counting on your discretion."

"Of course," Pru said in surprise. His eyes were like daggers as he watched her. He had that piercing stare down cold, she thought with a shiver.

"Within the next six months, we'll be losing an agent in SKURRT."

Her heart started to pound. "May I ask who?"

"His identity doesn't matter. Like I said, his departure isn't common knowledge and I'd like to keep it that way for now. The point is, we need to bring someone in ASAP, but frankly, finding the right candidate has been a challenge. This unit takes incredible dedication, Agent Dunlop."

"I'm aware of that, sir."

"Are you? I wonder," he murmured, his gaze cool and assessing. "It's not a job you leave behind when you go home at night. In fact, you don't ever leave it behind. You become the job, and the job becomes who you are. It's the first thing you think of when you wake up in the morning and the last thing on your mind before you fall asleep at night. And then you dream about it." He got up and walked over to the window, glancing out briefly before turning back to face her.

"You have to crawl inside some very dark minds, and when you come out, you'll never be the same again. And it'll eat at you. You'll become obsessed with every case that comes across your desk, especially the ones you can't solve, and there'll be a lot of those."

Pru wasn't certain if he expected a response or not, so she remained silent.

"This job changes you, and it changes how you react to the people closest to you. They won't understand that, and they'll resent you for it."

For one split second, as his gaze held hers, Pru saw what he meant. She saw what a toll the job had taken on him. The darkness in his eyes—in his soul—was like a glimpse into her future.

She suppressed a shudder, but she didn't turn away.

"I'll be honest with you. Your application is the strongest I've seen in a long time," he said.

A thrill raced up Pru's back. "Thank you."

"However, the fact that you're a woman troubles me. Not because I don't think you're up to the job. I have every confidence that you are. But the victims you see...most of them will be women. And that could make it more difficult for you."

"I can handle it, sir."

"That's what we all think." He walked back over to his desk and sat down. "All right," he said with a strange little sigh. "I'm going to give you your shot, Agent."

Pru couldn't help but smile. "Thank you, sir."

His answering smile seemed more like a grimace. "Wait ten years and see if you still want to thank me." He opened a drawer and pulled out a stack of folders. "Go over these case files tonight and be prepared to give me your assessment in the morning. We'll discuss it on our way to Huntsville."

Pru reached for the files. "Huntsville, sir?"

"I've arranged for us to interview an inmate, a convicted killer named John Allen Stiles. Ever heard of him?"

"He was dubbed the Casanova killer, in part because of certain items found at the crime scenes." Pru paused, frowning. "What's his connection to this case?"

"Read the files," Cahill said grimly. "And then you tell me."

Twilight fell softly over the University of Houston campus as Jessie Cahill hurried down the library steps. Panic skittered along her backbone. She never, ever went out alone after dark, but somehow she'd lost track of the time and that just wasn't like her.

She hesitated at the bottom of the steps, wondering if she should call Sarah. In the month and a half since school started, she and her roommate had become very good friends. Sarah would come to meet her if Jessie asked her to. She was that kind of person, but it wouldn't be fair to take advantage of her good nature. She had exams to worry about, too, and anyway, it was Jessie's own fault. She could have studied in the room rather than trudging to the library, but she found it hard to concentrate with all the noise in the hallways.

So, no, she wouldn't call Sarah because she didn't want to start using her friend as a crutch. She had to learn to stand on her own two feet. Besides, the campus was perfectly safe. She had nothing to worry about.

Still, as she adjusted her backpack to accommodate the weight of her books and her laptop, she had to resist the temptation to glance over her shoulder. But there was no one behind her. She was fine.

Except…she wasn't. Not really.

Maybe it was because she was on her own for the first time, but lately Jessie had been experiencing some of the old paranoia. And the night terrors had come back, too. She'd awakened screaming a few nights ago, terrified that when she opened her eyes, she'd see that evil, leering grin….

But instead, it had been her roommate leaning over her, gently shaking her awake. Sarah hadn't tried to get her to talk about the nightmare; instead, she'd turned on the television, made microwave popcorn and kept Jessie company until she'd finally stopped trembling. That was one of the reasons Jessie didn't complain when Sarah played music till all hours. She was the best friend Jessie ever had.

But Sarah wasn't there now to keep her company, and try as she might, Jessie couldn't shake the notion that someone was behind her. Following her. That *he* had somehow gotten out of prison and come for her.

That wasn't possible. Her dad would have told her. She was fine. She wasn't being followed.

She was fine.

Resisting the growing temptation to glance over her shoulder, Jessie cut across the campus toward her dorm. Even though it wasn't dark yet, the streets were almost deserted. U of H was a big commuter school, but the few people she met on the walkway nodded and smiled in such a friendly manner that Jessie began to feel better. Stronger. She was almost home. Only two more blocks....

As she rounded a corner, the hair at the back of her neck prickled. The sensation of being followed became so strong she couldn't ignore it. He was back there somewhere. She could feel him watching her.

Jessie tried to fight off the panic, but it gripped her so firmly she could hardly breathe. Her footsteps slowed as she turned to glance behind her.

She saw him at once.

He stood beneath a tree, one shoulder leaning

against the trunk while he tucked his hands into the pockets of his baggy jeans. He wore a baseball cap pulled low over his face so that Jessie couldn't see his features. He didn't wave, didn't nod. He just stood there.

Who was he?

It couldn't be *him.* It wasn't possible. He was in prison. He wouldn't get out for a very long time. Her dad had promised.

So who was he? And why was he following her?

Her heart pounding, Jessie whirled and ran smack into another student on the walkway. Muttering an apology, she kept her head bowed and hurried away.

All the way back to the dorm, she only looked back once, but she didn't see anyone behind her. Somehow that frightened her even more.

Running up the dorm steps, she burst through the front door, ignoring the curious stares from the kids watching TV in the lounge. She rode the elevator to the third floor, then trotted down the hallway to her room. Letting herself in, she shrugged out of her backpack and placed it on a nearby chair.

Sarah had left a note on her bed. She'd gone out with friends. If Jessie wanted to join them, she could call Sarah on her cell phone.

For a moment, Jessie considered doing just that. Maybe what she needed was to be around people. Listen to some music and have a good time. Act her age, for a change.

But who was she kidding? She wouldn't go out again tonight. Not by herself.

The room felt stuffy and she went over to open the window. Her heart skipped a beat when she glimpsed someone in the shadows below.

So what? she tried to tell herself. Whoever was down there was just someone who lived in the dorm. And maybe the guy under the tree had been waiting for someone. He was probably a student just like she was, and he hadn't been following her at all. She'd overreacted and now she'd left herself open to a panic attack.

Shoving the window down and locking it, she went over and sat down on the edge of her bed, trying to control her racing heart. Sweat beaded on her forehead and her chest tightened, as if a giant fist had closed around it.

She needed to call someone. She couldn't get through this by herself.

She wanted her mother so badly at that moment it was almost a physical pain, but she didn't want to call home. What if her mother's new boyfriend answered? Jessie wouldn't know what to say.

He seemed like a nice guy and all, but Jessie didn't want to talk to him. She didn't want to like him. She knew her attitude was immature, but she couldn't help it. Accepting that man into her life would be like betraying her dad.

Daddy, she cried inwardly. If she called, he would

come immediately. No questions asked. And Jessie didn't have to worry about someone she didn't like answering his phone. He was all alone.

But she wasn't sure she could handle seeing her dad tonight. Not because she didn't love him. She did. But she might not be strong enough to deal with the guilt that still haunted his eyes.

So she'd have to somehow get through this by herself. If she could just wait it out, Sarah would be back in a little while.

Lying down on the bed, Jessie hugged a pillow tightly to her chest as she squeezed her eyes closed.

She didn't want to think about that night, but she couldn't help it. It was always there. No matter how much time passed, she knew she would always see his face in every crowd, in every dream. Sometimes, like now, she could almost feel his knife pressed against her throat, his whispered warning that if she screamed, she would die.

He'd come in through her open window, and her mother, asleep in a room down the hall, hadn't heard a sound. Not until it was over.

But Jessie didn't blame her.

She and her mom had gone up to the lake house for the weekend, and her dad had promised to meet them after work. As usual, though, he'd been held up. If he'd been there, he could have saved her. He would have given his own life to protect her. Jessie knew that. She had no doubt about that.

But he hadn't been there, and Jessie didn't blame him, either, for what happened. She didn't have to. He blamed himself. She could see it in his eyes. And her mother blamed him, too, for not being there when he said he would be. For always putting work ahead of his family.

They'd divorced because of that night, because of Jessie. Sometimes the crushing weight of her own guilt was like a huge boulder pressing down on her chest.

Her cell phone rang, and she planned to ignore it. Then, thinking it might be Sarah, she reached for it with one hand while she wiped away her tears with the other.

"Sarah?" she said weakly.

A male voice laughed. "Do I sound like Sarah?"

Jessie trembled as she clutched the phone to her ear. "No, I…was expecting to hear from my room-mate, that's all."

"Disappointed?"

"No…" Jessie moistened her dry lips. Was she ready for this? She didn't know. She probably wasn't, but he was the first guy who'd caught her attention in a long, long time. The first one who didn't frighten her, didn't make her shudder in revulsion and dread when he looked at her.

"You sound a little strange," he said. "Are you okay?"

Jessie hesitated. "I don't know. I think I need to get out of this room."

"I was hoping you'd say that." He lowered his voice, deepening the tremor in her stomach. "So why don't we meet?"

She drew a shaky breath. "Where?"

"Same place as before. And Jessie?" he murmured. "Don't keep me waiting, okay?"

Chapter Four

"What are the four major classifications of serial killers?"

The question startled Pru, coming as it did so abruptly after twenty minutes of near silence. Cahill had barely spoken a word to her since they'd left the office, and Pru had found his taciturn demeanor a bit disconcerting at first. Then she'd decided that he was simply focused on maneuvering through the heavy road-construction traffic on I-45 and she shouldn't let his detachment get to her.

Once they passed the Spring exit, however, the freeway opened up, and he seemed to visibly relax.

"Well?"

"Is this a test?" she asked uneasily.

"I'm just making small talk."

Pru wasn't fooled. "Small talk is when you ask me what I did last night or what my favorite color is. I don't think you're making small talk."

He shrugged. "All right, then, call it a test. In any case, I'm still waiting for your answer."

Pru didn't hesitate. "The visionary-motive type killer is considered criminally insane...psychotic. They can be schizophrenic, mildly retarded and usually have low IQs. These are the guys who hear voices in their head telling them to kill. And they're the ones that if you meet them on the street, you immediately want to cross to the other side.

"The missionary-motive type killer wants to rid the world of whatever he perceives to be wrong or evil. The Green River Killer, for example, targeted prostitutes. He's distinct from the other types in that his need to kill is terminable. Once he fulfills his 'calling,' he can stop.

"The thrill killer murders for pleasure. It's a game for him. Unlike the visionary, he isn't mentally delusional. He doesn't have an unexplainable urge to take lives. He kills because he enjoys it. And because he thinks he can outsmart the cops.

"The last type is the lust-motivated killer. He kills because it turns him on sexually. Restraints, ritualism, fantasies and hatred of women are common in this type of killing. He derives erotic pleasure from torture, and the greater his victim's pain, the more aroused he becomes."

Rather than comment on what she'd said, Cahill asked another question. "Were you able to look over the files I gave you yesterday?"

"Yes, of course." Pru had been up past two studying those files. No way would she have faced Cahill this morning without being fully prepared. She wasn't about to blow the opportunity of a lifetime.

"Let's hear your thoughts, then."

"I made some notes…" Pru's briefcase rested on the floor at her feet. She bent to dig out her notebook, but Cahill stopped her.

"You don't need notes," he said curtly. "Just give me your overall impression."

His tone made Pru even more nervous, but she responded again without hesitation. "All right. I'll start with the similarities in all three cases. The victims—Ellie Markham, Tina Kerr and Clare McDonald—were young, blond, attractive and they lived in the same area of town, within miles of each other. Plus, they were all professionals. Ellie was a music producer for a local record company, Tina worked as a sales rep for a computer company and Clare was a lawyer. Since the police haven't been able to find a direct connection, either professionally or personally, we can probably rule out criminal enterprise, emotional, selfish or cause-specific intent."

He nodded. "What else?"

"The victims were murdered in their homes so that makes them low-risk targets. However, the Montrose area ups the ante somewhat, especially for sex-related crimes. If they were heavily into the underground club scene, then that could play a factor as well."

"Keep going."

"Okay, escalation. You have several months between the murders of Ellie Markham and Tina Kerr, but only a few weeks between Tina and Clare. The accelerated time frame could be an indication that the killer is losing control, but the meticulous condition of the crime scenes would seem to suggest otherwise. I'm inclined to think that it took him a while to get over the first kill. Once he got used to the idea, it became much easier for him."

"In which case, HPD can expect more bodies," Cahill said.

"Unless they can find him quickly," Pru agreed.

"Which classification would you put this guy into?"

Pru frowned. The question was tricky. "I'd rule out visionary because the organized nature of the crime scene indicates someone with an average to above-average IQ. I don't see these kills being missionary motivated, either, unless the police can come up with a common link among the victims, a nightclub they all three frequented, for example. A place the killer might deem as sinful."

"What about the third classification? A thrill killer?"

Pru shook her head. "I don't think so. Again, the crime scene is too organized and strangulation is a little too tame for these guys. They tend to like a lot of gore. So, by process of elimination, I'm left with the fourth classification, although I can't say I'm entirely comfortable with it, either. But the posing of the bodies—his signature—and the way he personalizes his victims are common traits among sexual killers."

Cahill shot her a glance. "What about the fact that none of the victims was sexually assaulted? Wouldn't that rule out a sexual killer?"

He was still testing her, but Pru didn't mind. "Not necessarily. This type of murderer has a sexual motive for killing, but it may or may not involve the act of sex. The killer will often take something from the victim, an object or even a body part, to help him later reenact the crime in order to achieve sexual gratification."

"Okay," Cahill said slowly. "So your conclusion is that we're dealing with an organized sexual predator."

"The signs are everywhere," Pru said. "This guy is all about planning. Everything he does is meticulous and well-thought-out. He leaves nothing to chance so he brings everything with him, including his own rape kit. And he doesn't leave anything behind…not the restraints, not the murder weapon and very little trace evidence. The pristine condition of the crime scene is part of an organized killer's personality. It's second nature to him." She paused, frowning. "There is a sticking point, though. An organized killer will usually dispose of the body in an effort to evade or delay discovery. Since that didn't happen here, it could mean we're dealing with a mixed personality or it could simply mean that transporting the body was too risky."

Cahill scowled at the road. "Or maybe he wants the bodies discovered."

"Yes, that's possible, too."

"Describe this guy for me, Agent."

"Well, from experience, we know that ninety percent of serial killers are male, and for sexual killers it's even higher. And their victims are almost always of the same race. So we can assume he's a white male, somewhere in his early twenties to early thirties. Like I said, he has an average to above-average IQ and is probably employed in a skilled profession. He's not a loner. He's socially and sexually competent, and will likely be living with a wife or girlfriend. He may use alcohol during the commission of the crime, and his kills are usually precipitated by some kind of stress. He's mobile. Although the fact that he's preying on women in the same neighborhood is an anomaly that frankly mystifies me. An organized predator will hunt for victims away from his hometown and his victims are almost always strangers. But this guy seems to be a stable killer. He may even live or work in the Montrose area."

She paused and stared out the window for a moment. "Another thing. It's not unusual for this type of killer to follow his crimes in the media, or even to take it upon himself to contact the police. And that brings me to the tape."

Cahill's mouth tightened. "Ah, yes, the tape."

"If he's the one who sent the tape to the police—

and I think he probably is—then it tells us a good deal
more about him. For one thing, he's done his research.
He knows something about serial killers. He goes
through all four classifications to make sure we know
he doesn't conform to any of them." Pru glanced at
Cahill. "But you already knew that, didn't you? That's
why you had me go through the list."

"'I don't hate women,'" Cahill quoted. "'Nor do I
take their lives for sadistic pleasure. I'm not on a mission. I'm not a thrill seeker. I don't hear voices inside
my head. I don't fit any of your profiles because I'm
not like any killer you've ever known.'"

The hair at the back of her neck lifted. Listening to
the killer's distorted voice alone in her apartment last
night had been unsettling enough, but to hear Cahill repeat those words was somehow even more disturbing.

"He's taunting us," Pru said. "He can't resist brag-
ging about how good he is. He wants attention, respect, and he damn well wants to make sure everyone
appreciates how clever he is."

"Traits of a thrill killer," Cahill pointed out.

Pru sighed. "I know. So the tape is another anomaly. Like I said, he's obviously done some research.
If he knows the general classifications, then it's probably a safe bet that he's also aware of the distinctions
between an organized and disorganized crime. That
could explain why he's so hard to pigeonhole. He
could be manipulating the MO, the crime scene, even
his own personality in order to mislead us."

"Very good, Agent," Cahill said approvingly.

Pru was allowed only a split second to bask in the glow of his praise.

"But there's a fifth classification that you failed to mention," he said. "It isn't as well documented, but the guys in the Investigative Support Unit at Quantico have been seeing it more often in recent years." They were approaching their exit and he automatically slowed. "Are you familiar with the term 'surrogate killer'?"

"Surrogate," Pru murmured. "As in replacement? Stand-in?"

Cahill nodded. "He kills under the orders or influence of someone else. The most famous case, of course, is Charles Manson."

Pru sucked in her breath as the purpose of their trip suddenly became crystal clear to her. That was why they were going to see Stiles.

She studied Cahill's profile as she digested the sudden revelation. "Do you really think John Allen Stiles could be manipulating someone to kill for him from his prison cell?"

Cahill shrugged. "I think it's entirely possible. Whether we can prove it or not is another matter."

Pru couldn't help shuddering, although she tried to mask it by leaning forward to retrieve something from her briefcase. Since her meeting with Cahill in his office yesterday, she'd done some research. John Allen Stiles had raped and murdered five young women in a three-month killing spree before the police had finally apprehended him. Somehow, according to the reports she'd read, he'd gotten to know his victims. He'd insinuated himself into their lives, and they'd become so infatuated with him that they'd willingly let him into their homes. One word that kept coming up in the descriptions of Stiles was *charismatic*. Another was *manipulative*.

The rose petals, candles and champagne found at the three recent crime scenes were disturbingly reminiscent of the murders Stiles had committed two years ago, as was the posing of the bodies with a long-stemmed rose.

And in just a little while, Pru would be coming face-to-face with him.

SURROUNDED BY PINE WOODS and a beautiful state park, Huntsville was like any other small East Texas town with one notable exception: it was known as the capital of the state's penal system. The area was home to seven separate correctional facilities including the infamous Walls Unit, which housed the state's only death chamber.

Pru had spent four years in Huntsville attending Sam Houston State University so she knew the importance of the prison system to the economy of the region. In time, like everyone else who lived and worked in the area, she'd gotten used to the sight of all those sprawling facilities enclosed by fences topped with razor wire.

But newcomers were often dumbfounded to discover that, rather than being in a remote location, the Walls Unit was right smack in the middle of town, surrounded by homes where people lived and raised their children.

In college, Pru's apartment had overlooked the thirty-two-foot-high wall, and the view often included protesters who came for nearly every execution. That was one thing Pru had never gotten used to nor would ever forget.

She and Cahill were expected at the prison, but they still had to go through the same procedure as every other visitor. Guards with mirrored poles checked beneath their vehicle, and their credentials were thoroughly scrutinized. Once they signed in and relinquished their weapons, they passed through a metal detector and then a uniformed guard escorted them to the warden's office.

Jim Pickett was a middle-aged man with sandy-colored hair and a thick, neatly trimmed mustache. He was only around five foot six or so with a thin, wiry build that seemed to exude nervous energy. He shook hands with both of them and as his gaze met Pru's, his eyes sparkled with what she might have assumed was good humor if not for the furrows in his brow and the deep grooves around his mouth and eyes. He had a tough job and it showed.

He motioned them to chairs across from his desk and then wasted no time in getting down to business.

"You're here to see John Allen Stiles." Taking a file from a drawer, he slipped on his glasses and perused the contents of the folder. "I took the liberty of doing a little research after we spoke on the phone, Special Agent Cahill. Since Stiles's transfer from the Harris County Jail eighteen months ago, he's been a model prisoner. No fights, no gangs, no trouble whatsoever."

"What about visitors?" Cahill asked. "We're interested in anyone on the outside he may have been in contact with."

"I had someone check the logs after you called. The only visitor he's had other than the chaplain is his sister, Naomi Willis. She comes every two weeks, rain or shine. And then, of course, his attorney. He's got a new one to handle his appeal. A man named Hathaway. Jared Hathaway. He's out of Houston, I think."

The name sounded vaguely familiar to Pru, but she couldn't place it at the moment.

"What about phone calls?" Cahill asked.

"You know the drill. Unless privileges are revoked, each inmate gets a limited number of phone calls per month, and they're monitored."

"Our San Antonio office recently traced a series of cell phone calls to and from the Ellis Unit," Cahill told him. "We know cell phones are a problem in prisons. Is it possible Stiles could have gotten his hands on one?"

Pickett's gaze was very direct. "Anything's possible. And you're right. Cell phones are a huge problem for us. It used to be that the contraband we worried about was drugs and weapons. Now it's cell phones, and I can guarantee these guys aren't using them to call home on Christmas or Mother's Day. You catch an inmate with a phone, though, and he'll flush it before you can ever lay a hand on it. And the pressure in those toilets…well, let's just say…you don't want to have an arm anywhere near one. Last time the FBI came looking, we had to drag the sewer. Those boys were raking out cell phones like pulling bass out of a lake."

"How do they smuggle them in?" Pru asked.

Pickett shrugged. "Any number of ways. Nobody likes to talk about it, but we had a guard not too long ago that was bringing them in. You get someone like that in here…not too bright, not too educated. He's working for little more than minimum wage, and these inmates…they know how to sucker people. They're experts when it comes to manipulation. They'll bribe someone or feed them a hard luck story. You'd be surprised how many people fall for it."

"What about the Internet? E-mail?" Cahill asked.

Pickett shrugged. "No inmate in the Texas prison system is allowed to use the Internet. But just like cell phones, that doesn't mean they don't have access. A lot of these guys have taken to cyberspace like ducks to water, and they know how to get around the system. What they do, see, is snail-mail

their information to friends or activists on the outside who forward it on to prisoner pen pal sites.
They set up an account and then the mail starts pouring in.

"Some of the inmates are legitimately reaching
out because they're bored and looking to make the
time pass faster, but a lot of them run scams. They por-
tray themselves on these Web sites as innocent,
abused, misunderstood individuals just looking for a
friend, a sympathetic ear, what have you. And the
people that buy into their sob stories are usually
lonely, vulnerable women who think they can reha-
bilitate these guys with a little TLC."

Pickett shook his head in disgust. "These inmates…most of them don't have a conscience. Right
and wrong don't mean anything to them. That's why
they're in here. They'll fleece some poor, unsuspect-
ing woman out of thousands of dollars and not blink
an eye."

"And there's no way to monitor these Web sites,"
Pru said.

"It's damn near impossible," he agreed. "There are
hundreds, maybe thousands, of them worldwide.
Searching each and every one for inmate ads would
require a full-time team of investigators. Same goes
for separating Internet-generated mail from regular
mail. It can't be done because we aren't allowed to
open ninety percent of what comes in here."

"So, in other words," Cahill said, "Stiles could

maintain regular contact with someone on the outside, and no one here would ever be the wiser."

Pickett gave them a thin smile. "That's the reality of it. Not a damn thing we can do about it, either."

Chapter Five

Rather than using one of the visitor's booths, Pickett had arranged for Pru and Cahill to interview Stiles in a small interrogation room equipped with a two-way mirror. The only furniture in the cinder-block space was a rectangular table and three straight-backed chairs. One chair was placed at the far end of the table, facing the two-way mirror, and the other two occupied the opposite end.

Pru and Cahill took their seats, and after about five minutes, the door opened and two guards escorted Stiles into the room. He wore the regulation orange jumpsuit with his inmate number stamped above the left breast and across the back. A chain connected the cuffs around his wrist to the shackles around his ankles, causing him to walk with a slow, awkward gait.

At first glance, there was nothing extraordinary about the man at all. In his early thirties, he had brown hair, blue eyes, and he was shorter than either of the guards, probably two or three inches less than six feet. The jumpsuit was so ill-fitting, it was hard to tell about his build, but his face was thin, his shoulders narrow. He looked almost fragile, and other than prominent cheekbones, completely nondescript.

He certainly didn't appear to be a Casanova type, a man capable of attracting the intelligent, professional women who had ultimately become his victims.

That was Pru's initial impression, but the moment his gaze met hers, she understood. The impact exploded deep inside her gut, and she almost gasped. It was as if he'd momentarily sucked all the air from the room, leaving her breathless and chilled. And yet, when he smiled at her, Pru couldn't tear her gaze away.

The word used to describe him in the reports she'd read flashed through her head. Charismatic.

Oh, yes. John Allen Stiles was charismatic to the extreme, although Pru wasn't sure that completely explained her reaction to him.

She found herself staring into the eyes of a brutal killer, and she couldn't look away.

The sensation was terrifying.

Cold sweat broke out along her forehead as her heart pounded inside her chest. For a moment, Pru wanted more than anything to get up and flee his presence. She didn't want that man looking at her. She didn't want to breathe the same air he breathed. If there was such a thing as true evil, Pru believed she'd just come face-to-face with it.

She moistened her lips, willing away her panic.

She couldn't let him see how he affected her because he would find a way to use it against her. He knew how to manipulate women. He was a master, and she couldn't lose sight of what he had done in the past. What he might still be capable of orchestrating from his prison cell.

He eased himself into the chair at the opposite end of the table from Pru and Cahill. He appeared perfectly calm. No telltale twitches. No darting eyes. He seemed to be in his element and enjoying it.

One of the guards stationed himself directly behind Stiles while the other moved to the door. Stiles tracked the second guard with apparent amusement before bringing his focus back to Pru. She tried to suppress a shudder as their gazes connected yet again.

He smiled. Knowingly. Charmingly.

"How good of you to come and see me," he said.

He might have been welcoming her into his parlor, so cordial was his tone. His voice was low and well modulated. He was an intelligent, educated man who liked to kill.

Beside her, Cahill sat perfectly still. He, too, seemed calm. If he experienced any of what Pru had felt when Stiles entered the room, he didn't show it. His voice, when he spoke, was just as pleasant, although there was an edge of something in his tone that also made Pru shiver.

"I'm Special Agent Cahill and this is Special Agent Dunlop."

Stiles lifted a brow. "The FBI? Well, well, well. To what do I owe this honor?"

"We'd like to ask you a few questions," Cahill said, still in that same matter-of-fact tone. "But first I'd like to show you some pictures." He pulled photographs of the three recent victims from his pocket and placed them on the table. "I want you to tell me if you recognize any of these women."

Stiles smirked. "Are they dead or alive, Agent Cahill?"

"They were alive when these pictures were taken."

"Ah." Something gleamed in Stiles's eyes. Pru almost expected him to smack his lips. "I confess, you have me intrigued. What happened to them?"

"They were strangled. They were each found clutching a single red rose. Sound familiar?"

Stiles shrugged. "Well, you know what they say. Imitation is the sincerest form of flattery. I'm puzzled, though. Why would you think I'd recognize them? Surely you don't think I had anything to do with their demise?" He held up his shackled hands. "As you can see, I'm a bit indisposed at the moment."

"Where there's a will, there's a way." Cahill shoved the pictures away from him, then nodded to the guard at the door. The man came over and slid the pictures down to Stiles.

"Just take a look." Cahill's voice was still controlled and unthreatening. "Tell me what you think."

"Of course. I'm happy to oblige in any way I can."

But Stiles made no move to pick up the pictures or even glance at them. Instead, his gaze moved back to Pru. She suspected he'd sensed her nervousness and was entertained by it. "I do have one stipulation, however."

Cahill never altered his tone or expression. "And that is?"

"I want to speak to Agent Dunlop. Alone, if you don't mind. In fact, you can leave now, Agent Cahill. You and I are finished."

"Let's not make this difficult," Cahill said. "Take a look at the pictures."

"You have my terms." And just like that, the mask of a refined, affable gentleman dropped, allowing Pru a terrifying glimpse of the sadistic monster hiding inside. His blue eyes turned icy, and there was nothing human behind them. Certainly no conscience. No remorse. He'd brutally raped and murdered five women, and those eyes were the last thing his victims had seen before they died.

Pru dropped her gaze. She had to clasp her hands tightly in her lap to keep them from trembling.

"Why don't you let your partner speak for herself?" Stiles suggested. "What do you say, Agent Dunlop? It'd be a pity if you made the trip all the way up here for nothing. All you have to do is agree to a nice little tête-à-tête with me, and then I'll look at your pictures. I'll tell you everything I know about them. You have my word."

Pru wasn't quite sure how she managed it, but she shrugged and looked him in the eyes as she said with cool indifference, "If that's what it takes."

He smiled. "I knew you'd see things my way. Agent Cahill? I believe you've been outmaneuvered."

Cahill hesitated, then stood. "I'll be right outside if you need me."

"How chivalrous," Stiles taunted. When the door closed behind Cahill, he returned his gaze to Pru. "Alone at last."

Pru glanced at the guard behind him. "Not quite."

"Just ignore them," Stiles said. "After a while you won't even notice they're there."

"Will you look at the pictures now?" Pru asked him.

"We haven't had our chat yet."

"Please look at the pictures, Mr. Stiles."

Something dark glinted in his eyes. "That wasn't the deal. If you want me to act in good faith, then I'm afraid you'll be held to the same standard."

She drew a breath. "What do you want to talk about?"

"You, of course."

"I didn't agree to that," she snapped.

He made a clucking sound. "Relax. I won't ask anything too personal."

She tried not to shudder as his gaze raked over her. "What do you want to know?"

"Tell me your first name."

"It's Prudence."

He gave a delighted laugh. "How charmingly old-fashioned. Is it a family name?"

"No. My mother is a Beatles fan."

"Ah, your mother." He sat back in his chair, his smile turning enigmatic. "Tell me about her."

"I'm not going to talk about my mother."

He sighed. "We can't talk about you, we can't talk about your mother. I'm losing my patience with you, dear Prudence."

She tried to control the shivers tracing up and down her spine. "Why can't we talk about the pictures?"

"We will, I promise. I'm a man of my word. Just answer one question about your mother." Slowly, he licked his lips. "Is she a natural blonde, too?"

Pru's stomach roiled. "I beg your pardon?"

"I prefer blondes. They're my weakness, you might say." He cocked his head. "It's a shame that you feel you have to disguise your true nature. That is why you color your hair, isn't it? To fool people into thinking you're something that you're not."

Beneath the table, Pru's hands were clammy with sweat. "A lot of people color their hair."

"Very few natural blondes dye their hair that unattractive mousy brown," he said with a disapproving frown. "Why do you?"

She didn't want to answer him, but she had no choice. It was obvious he had no intention of cooperating until he'd had his fun. "I guess I never felt like a blonde."

"Or is it because you're afraid if you let people see

the real you, no one will take you seriously?" He gave her a sympathetic smile. "A pretty, blond agent would undoubtedly have a hard time getting the respect she deserves, so you've found a way to adapt to your hostile environment."

Pru was startled by his insight. She winced at how close to home he'd struck.

"I see I've hit a nerve," he murmured. "You have very expressive eyes. Far more revealing than you know. I could tell what you were thinking the moment I first saw you with Agent Cahill." He paused, his own eyes mocking her. "Does he know, by the way?"

Pru swallowed. "What do you mean?"

"Agent Cahill. Does he know?"

She wanted to believe he was still talking about her hair color, but somehow she knew that he wasn't. Her face colored and he laughed at her. "Don't worry. Your secret is safe with me."

CAHILL GLANCED at Pru as they headed south on I-45 toward Houston. She still looked a little shaken by her meeting with Stiles, and Cahill couldn't say that he blamed her. He had listened to her private interview from the room behind the two-way mirror. It had been a hell of an initiation. Not every day, even in this job, that one had to confront a monster.

She'd barely spoken since they left the prison. As soon as they got back to the car, she took out her laptop and had been busily writing up her notes ever since.

Cahill studied her profile as she scowled at the computer screen. For some reason, her furrowed brow made her seem young and inexperienced, although she was neither. She was twenty-eight years old, and she had five years of experience and glowing performance reports under her belt.

Cahill was still confident in his choice, but only time would tell whether his instincts about her had been right. His decision yesterday to approve her transfer had probably seemed impulsive to her, but in fact, nothing could have been further from the truth. He'd studied her résumé for weeks. He'd talked to her supervisors, past and present, and a number of agents with whom she'd worked closely in the past five years in order to determine if she had the personality and the emotional fortitude required of the job.

He'd come away from all the interviews with the impression of an intelligent, focused, extremely dedicated young woman who was grounded professionally and personally. He liked what he'd heard about her and, in spite of her nervousness today, he thought she'd acquitted herself well with Stiles.

She was also attractive and that could work for or against her, depending on the circumstances. And her perspective, he supposed. It wasn't so much that she was pretty, but she had an interesting, intelligent face. Stiles had picked up on that, too. He seemed intrigued by her, and that could prove useful in the future.

Taking his gaze from the road, Cahill gave her another quick assessment. She had a gorgeous complexion, nearly flawless from what he could tell, and clear blue eyes, the kind of crystalline color normally associated with someone very fair.

He glanced at her brown hair. It was pulled back and fastened in the back with a clip. She looked fine to him, but he could tell she wasn't the type to primp or fuss with her appearance. Her simple black jacket and slacks looked as if they'd been chosen as much for comfort as style.

As if sensing his perusal, she glanced up and caught him staring at her. Their gazes collided and something twisted inside Cahill's gut.

Whoa, he thought. He hadn't expected that.

"Am I bothering you?" she asked suddenly.

He almost choked. "I beg your pardon?"

"Here I am, typing away, oblivious to everything else. I can see how that might seem rude." She gave him an apologetic smile. "I just wanted to record my first impression of Stiles before I lost something."

"That's a good idea." He cleared his throat. "You aren't bothering me."

"Good." She glanced away, then her gaze reluctantly came back. "What he said back there…when he asked if you knew…" She bit her lip, plainly uncomfortable with whatever was on her mind. "Maybe we should clear the air about that."

"You mean what he said about your hair?" Cahill didn't give a damn if she colored her hair, although he did wonder why she seemed so ill at ease about it. His ex-wife used to drop a small fortune every time she visited her stylist.

"My...hair?" She looked startled, then relieved. "Uh, yeah. That's what I meant."

Cahill shrugged. "As long as it doesn't interfere with your work, I don't care what color you dye it."

"It's just...Stiles seemed so fixated on it."

"Now that part does trouble me," Cahill admitted. His gaze went to her hair. "How the hell could he tell that you're a natural blonde? Are you, by the way?"

"Yes," she admitted grudgingly. "And I don't know how he knew. Maybe he could tell by my skin tone. Or maybe it was just a good guess. I don't know. I just wish he'd been as focused on those pictures. He barely glanced at them. I couldn't get anything out of him," she said with obvious disappointment.

"On the contrary," Cahill said. "He told us a great deal. Did you catch what he said about our driving 'up' to Huntsville to see him? How did he know we weren't driving 'down' from Dallas? He assumed we were from the Houston office because he anticipated why we were there."

"Because he already knew about the murders, you mean."

"That's my guess. And maybe the reason he didn't seem interested in the pictures is because he'd already seen them."

"Even if that's true, I'm not sure it would prove

anything," Pru said. "The victims' photographs were on the news."

Cahill rubbed the back of his neck. "I've been thinking about the Web sites Pickett mentioned. He said the inmates set up an account and the mail starts pouring in. If those women are willing to send money to someone like Stiles, it stands to reason they'd also send photographs of themselves."

"And he chooses his surrogate's victims from among his pen pals?" Her tone sounded a little incredulous. "I don't know, Agent Cahill. All the victims were successful, independent women. I can't see someone like Clare McDonald striking up a pen pal relationship with a convicted murderer."

"Can you see her letting a killer into her life and into her home?" he asked bluntly. "All of the victims were vulnerable in some way, and whoever killed them knew how to play on their weaknesses."

She shrugged noncommittally, but he could tell she wasn't yet convinced of his theory. And that was fine. It was just that…a theory. For now.

"When we get back to the office, I want you to find out whatever you can about those Web sites," he said. "Who runs them, how they're funded and so on."

She nodded. "I'm on it. Sir…what about the P.I. firm I told you about yesterday? The one that designs coincidences. If someone hired that agency to investigate Clare, then that could be a significant lead, especially if we can find a connection to the other two victims."

"Agreed."

"So...I should follow up?" she asked cautiously.

"You'll need some help. Do you know Tim Sessions?"

Wariness flickered in her eyes. "Yes...I know him. We've worked together before."

Cahill wondered about her guardedness, but he let it pass. "Good. Then you know he's an excellent tech. I want you to take him with you to Clare McDonald's office and have him go over her computer. The police confiscated her laptop, but they may not have had a chance to get by her office yet."

"Yes, sir." She hesitated again. "I need to ask you a question. Just so I'm clear on procedure. This is still technically HPD's case, right?"

"They asked for our support, and we're giving it to them," Cahill said with a frown. "Is that clear enough?"

"Yes, of course."

"Aren't you the one who pointed out a possible conflict of interest with HPD?" he reminded her.

"Yes, but you know as well as I do that some of the detectives are going to resent our involvement in the investigation."

"By some, you mean Janet Stryker."

Pru shrugged. "I didn't get the impression that she's exactly eager to cooperate."

"I'll coordinate with HPD, Agent Dunlop. You just do your job and let me worry about Sgt. Stryker."

Her features froze at his abrasive tone. "Yes, sir."

Cahill hadn't meant to come off as such an arrogant ass, but he didn't bother to apologize. If Agent Dunlop could deal with someone like Stiles, she could damn well learn to put up with his bad disposition.

"SO WHY DID YOU WANT this transfer?" Cahill asked a little while later. They were nearing Houston, and he decided it was time to offer an olive branch. She'd been staring out the window for the past half hour.

She gave him a suspicious look. "Is this another test?"

He almost smiled. "No. It really is small talk this time. How long have you been interested in SKURRT?"

"Since its inception eight years ago."

He glanced at her in surprise. "You must have still been in college. How did you even know about it?"

"I was a Criminal Justice major, remember? We talked about it in class, plus I discussed it with my dad." The tension seemed to seep out of her bit by bit. She sat back against the seat and folded her arms. "He knew I wanted to be in the FBI since I was fifteen years old."

"What did he think about that?"

"If he had reservations, he kept them to himself. He never once tried to change my mind. It wouldn't have done any good anyway. Besides, he knew I was doing it for the right reasons. I wasn't trying to follow in his footsteps, be the son he never had, or whatever. Not that he wasn't a great role model. I've always admired him. When I was growing up, he and the other special agents I knew were my rock stars." Her tone turned rueful. "Well, maybe rock star is the wrong term. They were more like superheroes to me."

"That sounds like a pretty big image to live up to," Cahill said dryly.

She smiled, displaying a single dimple at the left corner of her mouth. "Is it wrong of me to think John Douglas is cooler than Brad Pitt?"

"Brad might think so."

She laughed, and Cahill thought with a pang that it had been a long time since he'd heard that sound. It had been a long time since he'd met anyone like Agent Dunlop. Unless she'd fooled him, her dedication was genuine, her motives completely altruistic.

A real crusader, he thought, not without admiration.

"What about you?" she asked. "Are you a legacy?"

"No." He fiddled with the air conditioner for a moment. "My dad operated a charter fishing boat out of Galveston. He didn't make much money, but he was probably the most contented man I ever knew. I wouldn't have minded following in his footsteps, but I never could get my sea legs. I used to crew for him during my summer breaks, and I'd get sick as a dog every time we went out."

"I can see how that would pose a problem," Pru said sympathetically. "So how did you end up at the FBI?"

"I was in my first year of law school, married with

a new baby and bills piling up. The Bureau had a recruiter on campus one day. He gave me an application, I sent it in, and six months later, I was at the academy." He shrugged.

She looked a little crestfallen by the story. "That's it? You never even considered it before?"

"Unlike you, being a fed wasn't a lifelong ambition. I just needed to support my family." He glanced at her. "I'm not one of your superheroes, Agent Dunlop."

"Are you kidding?" She turned in her seat to face him. "I still remember the class you taught while I was at the academy. You held us all enthralled. I wanted to be just like you…" She trailed off, then added, almost shyly, "You're practically a legend. You realize that, don't you?"

He grimaced. "God, how old does that make me sound?"

"Old?" She looked stricken. "That's not what I meant at all. Your career…it's inspirational. I'm honored to be working with you."

The words were so sincerely spoken and she looked so earnest that Cahill was humbled. It wasn't a feeling he often experienced. Frustrated, yes. Even helpless at times. But humble was a new one.

Their gazes connected again, and the way she looked at him made him catch his breath. He felt that punch of attraction he'd experienced earlier, only stronger this time, and he wondered suddenly if he'd made a terrible mistake with Agent Dunlop.

Chapter Six

On first glance, Tim Sessions looked like the quintessential computer geek—tall and lanky with shaggy brown hair, dark-rimmed glasses and a blatant disregard for fashion.

After that initial impression, however, one noticed the humor and curiosity glinting in his gray eyes and the effortless way he carried himself, as if completely comfortable in his own skin. Even his wardrobe made sense once you got to know him.

When Cahill had asked if she knew Tim, Pru had purposely failed to mention that she'd gone out for drinks with him a couple of times. Nothing had come of it. They'd simply been two colleagues unwinding after a long day of work, so there was really nothing to tell.

Still, Pru wondered what Cahill's reaction would be if he knew. And she also wondered about the real reason she'd withheld the information. How simple it would have been to say in a breezy manner, "Yeah, I know Tim. We've had drinks after work a couple of times." She couldn't bring it up now, though. It would be too awkward and would make her seem as if she were trying to cover for something.

Pru wanted to mull over the dilemma for a while, but Tim was in such a talkative mood all the way downtown that she didn't have a chance to brood. Which was probably a good thing, she decided as they rode the escalator up from the tunnels to the glass-and-granite lobby of the Texas National Bank Building.

Linney, Gardner and Braddock occupied two of the upper-level floors in one of the tallest skyscrapers in downtown Houston. As Pru and Tim got off the elevator on the seventy-eighth floor, she was struck immediately by the view through the wall of windows in the reception area.

The space-age skyline melded so seamlessly with the decor, Pru felt as if she had stepped onto the set of a futuristic movie. The design was sleek, stark and modern, and the young woman seated behind the glass and brushed stainless-steel desk might have been a Hollywood starlet, she was that attractive. Her black, formfitting dress provided a dramatic contrast to hair so pale it could almost have been called platinum. She wore it swept back from her face, highlighting her stunning bone structure. Her makeup was flawless, her demeanor almost robotic as she watched them approach her desk.

"May I help you?" she asked with a cool, dismissive smile.

"I'm Special Agent Dunlop and this is Special Agent Sessions. We're federal agents," Pru said, whipping out her identification. "We're here regarding the murder of one of your associates...Clare McDonald."

The woman's perfectly arched brows lifted. "Clare? But the police have already been here. We've already told them everything we know."

"We'd like to have a look around her office," Pru said.

The woman worried her glossed lip. She seemed nervous, but that wasn't unusual. The sudden appearance of FBI agents was always a little unsettling.

Her hand fluttered to her throat, and Pru absently noticed her French manicure. Tasteful and elegant, like everything else about her. "If you would care to take a seat, I'll notify my supervisor that you're here."

"Thank you." Pru and Tim moved away from the desk.

He whistled as he glanced around. "Some place."

Pru nodded. "They probably don't even need air-conditioning, this place is so cold."

"Not to mention the receptionist's attitude." He gave a fake shudder.

High heels clicked down the granite hallway, and Pru turned to see a woman enter the reception area. She was an older and, if possible, blonder version of the receptionist. Slender, stately and elegant, she came forward and offered her hand.

"I'm Miriam Taylor," she said. "I understand you're with the FBI."

Pru made the introductions as they once again presented their identification. "We'd like to see Clare McDonald's office."

"Of course," the woman said in a carefully refined tone. "Her office is right this way." She beckoned toward the hallway, and the two of them followed her past a series of ornate, frosted glass doors through which Pru caught glimpses of color and movement.

Toward the end of the hallway, Miriam Taylor paused to unlock one of the doors. She opened it, then stepped back for Pru and Tim to enter.

Pru was surprised by the cramped, bleak quarters. Obviously the design allowance had been poured into the reception area and probably into the senior partners' offices upstairs. The lower-level staff, like Clare, had to settle for inexpensive furnishings and plain white walls.

"As Jade undoubtedly informed you, the police have already been here. I can't imagine what you still hope to find."

Pru's gaze went to the bare credenza behind Clare's desk. "Did the police take her computer?"

Miriam Taylor pursed her red lips in disapproval. "Yes, along with a number of other items that I'm afraid we may never recover. I can get you a list if you like."

"Thank you. That would be helpful."

Miriam started to leave, then stopped and whirled to face them. "There is one thing. I don't know if it's important."

"Everything is important at this point," Pru said. "What is it?"

"You asked about her computer..." Miriam's gaze darted about the office. "I'm sure you've noticed that the offices on this level are a bit...compact. Clare would sometimes go into one of the conference rooms to work because she claimed she was claustrophobic. The one she used most often is equipped with a computer. I have no idea what you're looking for, but it's possible she may have used the machine from time to time."

"Did you mention this to the police?" Pru asked.

"No, I'm sorry. It slipped my mind until now. The police came on Wednesday...the day of Clare's funeral. I'm afraid we were all a bit distracted."

"I understand," Pru said.

Beside her, Tim said, "Will I need a password to log on?"

"Not for that machine, no. It's used primarily for research. No one stores case-sensitive materials on it."

"In other words—" Tim's voice grew solemn "—if one of your associates or partners wanted to download Internet porn, you wouldn't be able to trace it back to the user."

"Internet porn?" Miriam's hand flew to her chest. Her nails, too, were perfectly manicured. "Surely, you don't think…" She looked horrified. "That can't be what you're looking for."

"It was a hypothetical question," Tim said.

She didn't bother to respond, but the look on her face gave him his hypothetical answer.

A FEW MINUTES LATER, Pru was alone in Clare's office. Tim had followed Miriam Taylor to the conference room, but Pru had stayed behind to have a look around. As she sat at the desk, she tried to picture Clare at work.

What had been her state of mind in the days and weeks leading up to her death? Had she become one of those lonely, vulnerable women so desperate for companionship that she'd blindly ignored the danger signs?

Pru remembered her conversation with Tiffany on the night of Clare's murder. She'd been beside herself with worry over Clare's recent behavior.

She's never been the secretive type, but now, suddenly, she won't tell me anything about this guy. Not his name, where he lives, what he does for a living. Nada. That's just not like her and you know it.

Why would Clare have kept the man's identity a secret from her best friend unless she'd known something was wrong with the relationship? Unless she'd anticipated Tiffany's disapproval?

Had John Allen Stiles been the new man in Clare's life?

The notion hit Pru like a fist in the gut.

What if Clare *had* been in contact with Stiles? What if she'd formed a pen pal relationship with him, and then he'd sent his emissary to kill her?

Pru still found it hard to believe that a woman like Clare could be so gullible, but she'd seen it before. Desperation and loneliness caused people to do foolish things.

A wave of regret washed over her as she sat at Clare's desk. They'd grown up in the same neighborhood, attended the same high school, but they hadn't been friends. Pru had never even really liked Clare. She and Tiffany had been the golden girls back then. It wasn't so much that Pru had envied their popularity; she simply hadn't had the patience or inclination to try to understand why it was so important to them. The things that seemed to fascinate girls like Clare and Tiffany—boys, makeup, clothes—had held little interest for Pru. Even at that age, she'd sensed there was more to life.

But by all indications, Clare and Tiffany had both grown into intelligent, successful, professional women, and as for herself, Pru certainly hoped she'd become a bit more tolerant. In time, they all three might have become friends, but they would never have that opportunity now. And that knowledge made Pru unexpectedly sad.

There was nothing she could do about that, though. She'd always believed that it was far more productive to concentrate on things within her control and so she began to systematically search through Clare's desk.

Since the police had been there before her, she didn't expect to turn up anything. She went through the motions anyway, and once she'd finished with the desk, she got up and walked over to the bookshelf. Scanning the titles—mostly professional journals— Pru was surprised to find a high school yearbook thrust between two weighty legal tomes.

That's odd, she thought. Why would Clare keep a copy of their old yearbook in her office?

Pru remembered something else Tiffany had told her on the night they'd met for drinks. She'd looked up a picture in the yearbook after a man claiming to be Todd Hollister, an old high school classmate, had approached her in the coffee shop asking questions about Clare.

According to the fingerprint match, that man had, in fact, been Danny Costello. Had the P.I. approached Clare with the same cover? Had she, too, been suspicious of his true identity?

Taking down the annual, Pru started to look up Hollister's picture, but the book fell open to a page that had been dog-eared.

On first glance, it seemed like a typical yearbook page with rows of class photos along with a few candid snapshots of some of the students.

One of the shots was of Clare and Tiffany. They stood in front of Clare's Mustang, smiling for the camera, looking more gorgeous and glamorous than two high school girls had any right to. With something of a shock, Pru realized that she'd been caught in the frame, too.

Her hair had still been blond then, and it was amazing how different she looked. Softer and more feminine somehow. Absently, she fingered a strand of hair as she gazed at the photo.

Unlike Clare and Tiffany, she seemed oblivious to the camera. Her head was bowed as she scowled at nothing in particular. She looked determined and intense, even at seventeen, and Pru thought, *No wonder I didn't have many dates.* She couldn't imagine what boys her age must have thought of her.

Her conversation with John Allen Stiles suddenly came back to her. He'd accused her of coloring her hair for fear she wouldn't be taken seriously as a blonde. His insight was chilling, and Pru wondered if he'd been able to tune in to his victims in much the same way. If his empathy had made them trust him.

"Agent Dunlop?"

She spun to find the receptionist, Jade, standing in the doorway. Pru had no idea how long she'd been there.

Shrugging apologetically, the woman said, "I didn't mean to startle you. Miriam wanted me to check and see if you needed anything."

"I'm fine. No, wait, on second thought, there is something you can do," Pru said when the young woman started to turn away. "Can you find out for me if a man named John Allen Stiles has ever been a client of this firm?"

The woman hesitated. "I suppose I can check the database, but I don't have authorization to get you any of the case files."

"I understand," Pru said. "Right now, all I need to know is whether or not Stiles has ever been represented by this law firm."

"I'll see what I can find out," the woman murmured.

She disappeared back to her station, and Pru continued her search of Clare's office. By the time she finished, she still hadn't heard back from the receptionist. She walked down the hall to the woman's desk.

"Were you able to find the information I asked for?"

Jade cast a nervous glance down the hallway. "I checked the database."

"And?"

She nodded. "Mr. Stiles is a client of this firm."

Pru lifted a brow. "*Is?* Meaning, in the present?"

"Yes."

"Who's his attorney?"

"Mr. Zellman is handling his appeal."

"Sid Zellman?"

"Yes, that's right."

The name shocked Pru, and she instantly thought back to what Tiffany had said about him. She'd mentioned his name in conjunction with Clare's suspicion that she was being followed.

"Wait a minute," Pru said. "The attorney on record at the prison where Stiles is incarcerated is a man named Jared Hathaway."

"Mr. Hathaway is one of our associates. He handles litigation for Mr. Zellman, as well as Mr. Zellman's outside appointments."

"Why is that?"

The receptionist moistened her lips as her hand crept to her throat. "I…really can't speak to their arrangement. Perhaps you'd like to talk to Miriam about it."

"I'd prefer to speak to either Mr. Hathaway or Mr. Zellman," Pru said firmly.

"Mr. Hathaway is on vacation. He won't be back for another week."

"What about Mr. Zellman?"

Jade's fingers plucked at her pearl necklace. "He doesn't see clients."

"I'm not a client. And maybe I should make myself clear." Pru gave the woman a cold, authoritative stare. "This isn't a request. Tell Mr. Zellman that the FBI is here to see him."

"Yes, of course…" Jade turned away from Pru as she picked up the phone. She murmured something into the mouthpiece that Pru couldn't distinguish, and then her voice rose as she met with obvious resistance. Hanging up the phone, she glanced at Pru. "Someone will be with you momentarily."

Pru nodded. "That's fine. But just so you know, I

have every intention of speaking with Mr. Zellman before I leave here."

The woman cast an uneasy glance toward the hallway as she sat down behind her desk. A few minutes later, when footsteps sounded near the reception area, she looked up in relief. "Here's Mr. Zellman's assistant now. He'll take you up."

The man who strode down the hall toward her was tall, thin, attractively groomed and expensively dressed. He wore a charcoal pin-striped suit paired with a white shirt and dove-gray tie. His blond hair was cut stylishly shaggy, and his complexion was so flawless, he almost appeared made up.

Another blonde, Pru thought. What was with this firm?

The man looked vaguely familiar to her, although she was almost certain they'd never met before. She wondered if he'd once been an actor or a model. Like the receptionist, he had the kind of features a camera would love.

He held out his hand. "Special Agent Dunlop? I'm Greg Oldman. You're here to see Mr. Zellman, I understand."

"Yes, I am," she said in a tone that conveyed both her impatience and determination.

"He's expecting you. I'll take you right up."

Well, that was a surprise, Pru thought. Judging from the receptionist's reluctance, she'd expected to meet with a much-practiced runaround, but Greg Oldman seemed to have no such intent. He led her down the hallway to an elevator that operated between the two floors occupied by the firm.

When they exited on the upper level, Pru once again had a feeling of stepping into another world. Rather than a futuristic movie set, however, the floor housing the senior partners' offices reeked of old money, good breeding and exquisite taste.

Greg Oldman led her down yet another hallway and as he opened a heavy oak door, he gallantly stepped aside to allow her to enter before him.

Pru stepped inside and glanced around. The outer office was as richly appointed as the lobby. The smell of leather and something more exotic permeated the air, and as Oldman brushed by her, she realized the scent was his cologne.

He crossed the room and once again beckoned her to follow. Pru's heels sank into carpeting so plush, her footsteps were completely silenced.

Oldman knocked softly on the door to the inner sanctum, waited a split second, then opened it enough to stick his head inside. "Mr. Zellman, Special Agent Dunlop is here to see you."

Pru couldn't hear the reply, but Oldman pushed the door open wide enough for her to pass through and motioned with his head for her to enter.

As she went by him, he murmured something in her ear that sounded like *allergies,* but Pru thought she must have misheard him.

PRU TRIED NOT TO APPEAR fazed by the surgical mask Sid Zellman wore over his mouth and nose.

He sat behind a mahogany desk so huge that she had difficulty judging his size. She concentrated on the features she could catalog: meaty hands folded on his desk, dark hair and glassy eyes that tracked her with such intensity that Pru felt the hair on the back of her neck lift.

"Mr. Zellman? I'm Special Agent Dunlop with the FBI. I'd like to ask you a few questions regarding one of your clients…John Allen Stiles."

He yanked down the mask, revealing an almost lipless mouth and a narrow, pointed nose. A generous description would not have called him pleasant-looking, but even apart from his appearance, Pru found him oddly repulsive.

"Mr. Stiles and I enjoy an attorney-client privilege." His voice was low and raspy, not at all the kind of voice that would be able to effectively argue a case in court. "But then, you know that."

"Yes, of course," Pru said. "I'll do my best not to ask you anything that would breach that confidence."

"You can ask," he said tersely. "I just won't answer."

"Fair enough." Pru smiled, trying to ease the palpable tension in the room. "Mr. Zellman, are you familiar with certain Web sites that run ads for inmates looking for pen pals?"

"I've heard of them."

"Do you know if your client has placed such an ad?"

"Why are you asking?" he demanded in that same harsh voice.

"Some of those ads are scams. Inmates use them to con innocent women out of money for their defenses." She glanced around. "I don't imagine your services come inexpensively."

He gave her a reproving look. "If you're asking how my fee is paid, Linney, Gardner and Braddock handles a lot of pro bono work, especially in cases where the client was so poorly represented at trial."

"You don't feel Stiles received a fair trial?"

Zellman gave a derisive snort. "It was a joke. The public defender actually fell asleep at one point during the trial. *Fell asleep,*" he said incredulously. "Does that sound like competent representation to you?"

"How did Mr. Stiles come to your attention?"

"As I said, our firm represents a lot of such cases. A friend of the court referred Mr. Stiles to us."

"How long have you been handling his appeal?"

"A few months."

"Do you know if Stiles ever came in contact with Clare McDonald?"

His brows rose as he wheezed. "Ah," he said. "Now we're getting to the heart of the matter, aren't we? Clare McDonald's murder. You want to know if my client had anything to do with it."

"How could he?" Pru said, playing devil's advocate. "Your client is behind bars."

"I'm not stupid, Agent Dunlop. Clare was strangled in her own home. Her body was posed in such a way as to emulate the crimes for which my client was convicted. It's not a reach to assume that you're here because you think there may be a connection."

Pru was taken aback by his candor. "The police have withheld the details of the crime scene from the public. How would you know anything about how her body was posed?"

His repellent mouth twisted in what Pru assumed was a smile. "I have friends in the police department, though admittedly, defense attorneys are somewhat persona non grata at 1200 Travis. Still, cops are the same as anyone else. They like to talk. They like to impress. I assure you, the posing of the body is common knowledge by now."

"Did you happen to mention this 'common knowledge' to your client?"

"Of course, I mentioned it," he said with a cavalier shrug. "It's relevant to his appeal."

"How so?"

"You aren't stupid, either, Agent Dunlop. Crimes that are almost identical to the ones for which my client was convicted are still being perpetrated. Three more young women have been killed while an innocent man sits in prison."

The evidence against Stiles may have been circumstantial, but Pru had looked into his eyes. She had spent time in the same room with him, and *innocent* was not a word she would use to describe him.

"Do you know of anyone, other than yourself and your associate, Mr. Hathaway, with whom Stiles may be in regular contact?"

"There's no one else that I know of. Except for his sister, Naomi, of course. A charming woman. Have you met her?"

"No, I haven't." But Pru intended to, as soon as possible. "One last question, Mr. Zellman."

He wheezed and slid the mask over his mouth and nose. With his other features hidden, his eyes seemed hawkish. Predatory.

"A few weeks before she was murdered, Clare confided to a friend that she thought she was being followed. Do you have any idea who it could have been?"

"How would I know that?" he asked through the mask.

"Because Clare thought it might have been you."

His eyes deepened as he regarded her for a long, pregnant moment, and then he tore off the mask and laughed.

"Did I say something funny?" Pru asked coolly.

"Yes, you did, Agent Dunlop. You have no idea."

"I'm afraid I fail to get the joke."

He stopped laughing and gave her a piercing stare. "Are you familiar with the condition known as agoraphobia?"

"The fear of leaving one's home."

"Not precisely the definition, but close enough," he said. "For reasons I won't go into, I suffer from a similar affliction. I have an apartment on another floor, and everything I require is brought to my door by either a delivery service or by my assistant, Mr. Oldman. You see, Agent Dunlop, I couldn't have been the one following Clare McDonald because I haven't left this building in over fifteen years."

Chapter Seven

Pru met Tim on the lower level and as they waited for the elevator, he said, *"Score,"* beneath his breath.

"You found something," Pru said with a surge of adrenaline.

He glanced over his shoulder at the frigid receptionist. "Yeah, but let's get out of here first. This place gives me the creeps."

"Gives *you* the creeps," Pru muttered as they stepped onto the elevator.

They waited until they were in the car heading back to the office to exchange information.

"You didn't really need me for this job," Tim said. "All I did was check the temporary Internet files stored on the hard drive. Someone used that computer to visit an inmate Web site called TheForgottenMan.com. But there's no way to tell if it was Clare McDonald."

"Did you go to the Web site?"

"Yeah, and it was pretty much the way you described it. A bunch of prisoners trolling for pen pals."

"What about Stiles? Did you see his ad?"

Tim shrugged. "No, but there were dozens. Hundreds, maybe. I didn't have time to go through them all. I'll take another look once we get back to the office." He glanced at Pru. "I don't suppose there's any way we could get our hands on Clare's personal computer?"

"Her laptop is still in police custody, and you know how territorial the locals are."

"What about the other two victims?"

"I don't know, but I'll see what I can find out. Cahill is coordinating the investigation with HPD. He can at least alert them what to look for on the hard drives."

"Yeah, well, good luck with that," Tim muttered.

She ignored his disdain for the technical expertise of the police department. His attitude wasn't uncommon in the Bureau. "One more thing I'd like you to do if you have time."

"Shoot."

"There's a private detective firm on South Post Oak called Tripp Investigations. The owner is Max Tripp, and from what I've been able to gather, he has a number of ex-cops working for him. I'm interested in one in particular, a man named Danny Costello." She explained about her suspicion that Costello may have been hired to follow Clare before her death. "Any information you can dig up about Tripp's agency would be a big help."

"I'll see what I can find."

Pru dropped him in front of the building and after he got out, he leaned back in through the open door.

"In case I forgot to mention it, congratulations on your transfer."

She smiled. "Thanks, Tim. It's something I've been wanting for a long time."

"You and a few dozen other people," he said ironically. "So, how is it working with the great one?"

"You mean Agent Cahill?" She tried not to let anything show on her face. "It's…a bit intimidating," she admitted.

"Well, don't let him get to you. I suspect his bark is a lot worse than his bite."

"I'll keep that in mind."

Tim nodded. "You do that. And in the meantime, if I turn up something on Stiles or Costello, where can I reach you?"

"I've got outside appointments for the rest of the day, and then I'm meeting my dad for dinner later. But I'll keep my cell phone turned on."

"Okay. Tell Charlie we need to get back out on the water one of these days real soon."

Pru wasn't surprised that Tim knew her father. Everyone in the Houston office seemed to know him. "I'll be sure and give him the message."

Tim grinned and shoved back a lock of shaggy hair. "You take care, Pru. And remember what I said about Cahill." Then, patting the top of her car, he turned and strolled off.

A FEW HOURS LATER, Pru glanced at the digital clock in her Subaru and muttered an oath. She was nearly half an hour late. As she pulled into the parking lot of Mo's Grill, just off South Main near the medical center, she spotted her father's blue SUV sitting beneath one of the massive crepe myrtle trees that edged the property.

For as long as Pru could remember, she and her father had been coming to Mo's. A tiny hole-in-the-wall restaurant that catered to a lot of the med students in the area, it was open around the clock, just the sort of place a broke, bleary-eyed resident could stumble into after a twenty-four hour shift.

The place was owned and operated by a sixty-year-old Guatemalan woman named Molena, a tiny redhead with the stamina and figure of someone half her age. She manned the cash register and supervised the waitstaff with a ruthless, drill-sergeant efficiency while her partner of nearly forty years, a fiery Cuban named Miguel, ran the kitchen. They lived in an apartment over the restaurant, but they weren't married and never had been. At least not to each other. Rumor had it that Miguel had once worked for Fidel Castro, and that he'd left a young bride behind when he fled the island country after becoming disillusioned with the revolution.

Whether any of that was true or not, Pru had no idea. But she'd always thought the exotic pair one of the most romantic couples she'd ever known, and she had a feeling that even now, although they were in their sixties, the ardor in their relationship had barely cooled.

Her father was already seated in their favorite

booth with a basket of chips and Mo's famous pineapple salsa to curb his appetite.

"Sorry I'm late," Pru murmured as she slid onto the bench opposite him. "I was held up at work."

"No need to apologize," he said with a shrug. "I know how it is."

That was one of the things she loved about being with her dad. There was no awkwardness. No resentment. No pressure of any kind. Just a nice, easy camaraderie.

He looked good, Pru thought with a surge of affection. He wore a light blue shirt that matched his eyes, and his hair, what was left of it, was freshly trimmed. In his midsixties, he was still fit and trim with the same ramrod posture he'd carried since his days as a Marine.

"Before I forget, Tim Sessions wanted me to tell you that the two of you need to get back on the water soon. I assume he meant fishing."

"Tim? How's he doing?" Her father poured her a glass of sangria as she reached for a chip.

"He seems to be doing fine," Pru said. "Why?"

Her father shrugged. "I don't know. I thought something might be developing between you two there for a while."

"Is that why you went fishing with him?" Pru asked suspiciously.

"I went fishing with him because he's a good guy and he happens to have a nice little houseboat down on the Gulf." Her father refilled his own glass. "But enough about Tim. Let's have a toast," he said with a twinkle in his eyes. "I heard about your transfer."

"That was fast. Who told you?"

"Doesn't matter." Touching his glass to hers, he said, "Congratulations, honey. I know this is what you've wanted for a long time."

She couldn't help beaming. "Thanks, Dad. I still can't believe it. It happened so fast."

He gave her a reproachful look. "Come on. You're not that naive."

"What? What do you mean?" she asked in surprise as she munched on a chip. "Okay, I know it wasn't really all that fast. It's been over a month since I submitted my request. But when I didn't hear anything, I assumed it had been turned down. Then I ran into John Cahill in the elevator yesterday, and I decided to ask him about it point-blank. We had a conversation in his office, and he ended up approving my request. That part *was* fast," she finished with a shrug. "And unexpected."

Her dad shook his head. "It may have seemed that way, but trust me, it wasn't. Cahill spent a lot of time checking you out, and that includes talking to your supervisors, colleagues, instructors at the academy and yours truly."

Pru stared at him in shock. "He talked to you? About me?"

He eyed her over the rim of his glass. "It was a fairly lengthy discussion."

Pru sat back against the booth. It was becoming extremely clear to her how her father had found out about her transfer so quickly. "What did you tell him?"

"What do you think?" He set his glass on the table. "I told him that, for personal reasons, I'd hoped you'd go into white collar crime, but, nevertheless, he'd be lucky to have you."

Pru grinned. "Thanks."

He shrugged as he dipped a chip into the salsa. "No thanks necessary. I meant every word of it."

"It's odd, though, that he talked to so many people, including you," she said accusingly. "And I knew nothing about it."

"Surely that doesn't really surprise you. John Cahill is a cautious man. He's particular about who he brings into SKURRT. Especially when it comes to picking his own replacement."

Pru's heart skipped a beat. "What do you mean his replacement?"

Her father continued to eat. "I hear he's leaving in six months."

Pru grabbed his hand as he reached for another chip. "Dad, stop eating for a minute and tell me what you mean. Cahill's leaving SKURRT?"

"He's leaving the Bureau. Retiring. He didn't tell you?"

Pru tried not to sound as stunned as she felt, but it was as if the wind had been knocked out of her. "He mentioned that they were losing a team member, but he didn't say who it was."

"Well, now you know. Can I eat?" her father grumbled.

But Pru couldn't let it go. "Do you have any idea why he's leaving?"

"Burnout would be my guess. It happens to all of us sooner or later, but in a unit like that…" He topped off their drinks. "Plus, I doubt he's ever gotten over what happened to his daughter."

Pru frowned. "Something happened to his daughter?"

"It was a couple of years ago. You were still in Washington, so you wouldn't have heard about it." He paused, his eyes going dark. "It was bad, honey. His wife and daughter went up to a house they had on Lake Conroe for the weekend. John was supposed to meet them, but he got delayed on a case. Someone broke into the house that night. Came in through the girl's bedroom window. He raped her at knifepoint while the mother was asleep down the hall."

Pru's hand flew to her mouth. "Oh, my God, Dad. That's awful."

He nodded. "Yeah, it was rough."

"Is she okay? John's daughter, I mean?" Pru barely even noticed that she'd used his first name. It came out so easily.

"I hear she's doing pretty well. She's in college now. University of Houston, I think."

"Did they find the guy who did it?"

"Yeah." He wiped his mouth with the napkin.

"After his arrest, a number of other women came forward. John's daughter didn't have to testify, which was a huge relief, I'm sure. The guy's doing twenty, but they'll be lucky if he serves half that. You know how the system works." He shook his head. "Poor kid. The last thing she needs is for that bastard to be out walking around on the streets."

"I had no idea," Pru murmured.

"No, you wouldn't. Cahill is a private kind of guy. I don't imagine he'd ever bring it up. Besides everything his daughter went through, there was all that stuff with his wife."

"What stuff with his wife?"

"The way I heard it, she blamed John for what happened."

Pru glanced up. "Why? He wasn't even there."

"That's precisely why. It's a man's duty to protect his family. You can argue about it until you're blue in the face," he said before she had a chance to. "But it doesn't have anything to do with a woman's independence. It's not chauvinistic. It's instinct."

They'd had this discussion before. Pru knew it did no good to argue, so she didn't even try. She sipped her drink and thought about everything her father had told her.

He leaned across the table, his expression stern. "I'm going to speak my mind about something and it's probably going to tick you off, but that's never stopped me before."

Pru sighed. "What is it?"

"Something's going on here that I don't much like. You get a look on your face every time you mention John Cahill's name. You can deny it all you want, but you've never been any good at hiding your feelings. You've got a thing for this guy." Her father shook his finger accusingly. "It's as clear to me as the nose on your face and unless you want to wreck your career, you'd better find a way to get it out of your system. The sooner, the better."

"Dad—"

"I'm not going to say another word about it." He picked up the menu. "You're a grown woman. You know what you have to do. Let's just order our dinner and enjoy the rest of the evening."

He took a long time perusing the entrées even though he always ordered the same thing. After a few minutes of quibbling over the pros and cons of each dish, they placed their orders and sat back to enjoy the sangria.

"Speaking of your mother…"

No one had said anything about her mother, but Pru didn't point that out. She was just glad to have the focus off her. "What about her?"

Her father studied his drink. "Have you seen her lately?"

His tone was casual, but he didn't fool Pru. She wasn't the only open book at their table. "We went to Clare McDonald's funeral together. Why?"

He seemed fascinated by his drink. "I was just wondering how she's doing. She seemed a little tired the last time I saw her."

"She's fine, Dad. But if you're worried about her, why don't you call her? Or better yet, drop by the store."

He glanced up with a frown. "I couldn't do that."

"Why not? You two were together for over thirty years. You don't have to stop caring about each other just because a piece of paper says you aren't married anymore."

His features set in stubborn resistance. "Your mother made her wishes perfectly clear. I'm not about to make a nuisance of myself."

"Oh, Dad." Pru shook her head.

"What?" he asked gruffly.

"Nothing. It's just…you're a fine one to talk, that's all."

CAHILL SETTLED into his easy chair—feet propped up, a drink on the table next to him—and pretended to relax. But he was still too wired. The conversation with Stiles kept playing over and over in his head, and Cahill found himself wondering, as he always did, if he'd failed to pick up on a clue, some nuance that would tell him they were on the right track.

Earlier, he'd spread the crime scene photos from the recent cases and from the Casanova murders across the dining room table and studied them until his eyes began to water and burn and he'd had to take a break.

The inconsistencies—anomalies, as Agent Dunlop had called them—baffled him, too. The crime scenes practically screamed an organized personality, but there had been no attempt to dispose of the bodies. No overkill. No torture or mutilation. The kills had been relatively clean.

The items found at the crime scenes—the champagne, candles, rose petals leading to the body—were identical to the murder scenes Stiles had left behind, as was the signature. The similarities couldn't be a coincidence, and yet Cahill's instincts had told him from the first that they were dealing with something other than a copycat.

That brought him back to a surrogate-type killer, but the tape that had been sent to the police was yet another inconsistency. Stiles had never taunted the police. Why would he have his replacement do so now?

Unless the surrogate was acting on his own.

I don't fit any of your profiles because I'm not like any killer you've ever known.

Cahill wiped a hand across his mouth. What the hell was this guy trying to tell them?

Once again, he went back over the conversation with Stiles. His lack of interest in the photos of the dead women. His assumption that they'd driven "up" to Huntsville. The way he'd tried to play Dunlop.

Stiles had picked up on her nervousness and he'd

tried to use it against her. Tried to rattle her. Dunlop was a good agent, but she wasn't without vulnerabilities. No one was.

Still, the more Cahill saw of her, the more impressed he became. She was a dedicated, diligent agent whose credentials far surpassed the other applicants—even Tim Sessions, whose technical expertise was unparalleled. Cahill hadn't seen anyone with Dunlop's potential in years, and if her transfer ruffled some feathers, so be it. She had all the right instincts, and that couldn't be taught in any class. It was a hard thing to explain to some of the excellent agents he'd had to turn down over the years, but the fact of the matter was, an agent either had a feel for this kind of work, or he didn't. Agent Dunlop had it, all right, and if she still retained some of her soft edges, the job would take care of that in time.

Every case would change her, harden her, make her view the world in ways she couldn't yet imagine. Cahill regretted that because he liked her.

There had been a moment or two in the car when he'd felt something even more for her. The attraction had taken him completely by surprise.

Nothing would come of it, of course. He'd see to that. Getting involved with another agent, especially a superior, could damage her career. It was a complication she didn't need and an aggravation he didn't want. In six months, he'd be out of there. It was time to move on, and he meant to make a clean break.

He needed to concentrate on his family for a change, although he supposed it was a little late for that. Lauren was no longer in the picture, but he felt surprisingly little regret over the divorce. It had been coming for a long time, and Jessie's attack had simply crystallized all the bitterness and resentment that had been simmering beneath the surface for years.

His daughter was his only concern now. He'd gone through a rough time when she'd decided to live in the dorms. She could easily have made the commute from her mother's home in the suburbs, but she'd wanted to be on her own and that worried Cahill. She still seemed so young, barely eighteen while a lot of the other freshmen were already turning nineteen.

But it had been her decision and as much as he'd been dying inside, Cahill had known better than to try and hold her back.

Still, there were times when it was all he could do not to drive to the university, grab her in his arms and hold her so tightly that no one would ever be able to hurt her again. It didn't matter how old she was or how far away she went, she would always be his little girl and he would always feel that overwhelming need to protect her. He couldn't help it.

He eyed the phone now, thinking that if he could just hear her voice, make sure she was okay, he might be able to turn in and get some sleep. He'd promised himself he wouldn't do that, though. He'd let her call him when she needed to. *If* she needed to.

But they hadn't talked in days....

He found himself calling her cell phone in spite of his resolve. When he got her voice mail, he left a brief message, then called the phone in her dorm room. A young woman picked up.

"This is John Cahill. Jessie's father. Is she there?"

"Oh, hey, Mr. Cahill. This is Sarah, her roommate. We met on move-in day, remember?"

An image of a freckle-faced redhead popped into his head. "Yes, of course, I remember. How are you, Sarah?"

"Fine, thanks."

"Is Jessie around?"

"No, I'm sorry, she's not here."

"Do you have any idea when she'll be back?"

"I just got in myself. She usually leaves a note, but I guess she forgot this time. She has a chemistry test tomorrow, so she's probably studying at the library. Do you want me to have her call you when she comes in?"

"No, that's okay. It's not an emergency. I just wanted to say hi."

"I'll tell her you called then."

"Thanks."

"Good night, Mr. Cahill."

"Good night."

Cahill hung up and polished off the remainder of his drink. If Jessie was studying at the library, then that would explain why she'd turned off her cell phone. There was no need to worry about her. Everything was fine.

So why did he suddenly feel so uneasy? Why did he have an almost uncontrollable urge to drive down to the campus and look for her himself?

Because you're an overbearing jerk, that's why.

Fixing himself another drink, he dropped his head against the back of the chair, closed his eyes and prayed for sleep.

Chapter Eight

Naomi Willis lived just off Washington and I-10 in one of the new town house complexes that had sprouted like mushrooms in the area. Whatever trees had been in the neighborhood had all been bulldozed to facilitate construction, and now the view from most of the units was of another building or a concrete parking lot.

As Cahill parked the car in front of Naomi's building, Pru glanced at his profile. He looked like hell this morning. The creases around his mouth seemed to have deepened since yesterday, and the dark circles under his eyes were a graphic manifestation of what must have been a sleepless night.

Pru wondered what had kept him up. The case or something personal?

She couldn't stop thinking about what her father had told her at dinner last night. Cahill's daughter had been raped, and he blamed himself for not being able to save her. Pru could understand that. Like her father, his protective instincts would run deep, but the ex-wife's attitude was a little harder to fathom. Her own guilt must have been overwhelming. Her daughter attacked while she slept…no wonder she'd lashed out at someone else. It had probably been her way of coping, but in reality neither she nor Cahill was at fault. No one was to blame except the monster that had come in through their daughter's bedroom window.

Cahill turned and caught her staring. Instead of glancing away, Pru said, "Are you okay?"

He scowled. "Why wouldn't I be?"

"I don't know. You seem a little distracted this morning."

He shrugged. "I didn't get much sleep last night."

"I kind of figured," Pru said.

His expression sharpened. "What do you mean by that?"

"I mean, this case is keeping me awake, too. I couldn't stop thinking about it last night."

He gave her a halfhearted smile, as if reading her mind. "Should I say I told you so?"

"You can if you want to." She lifted one shoulder. "But lucky for me, I don't need much sleep."

"Another point in your favor," he murmured as he opened his car door.

Another point in her favor? What did that mean? Pru wondered.

They headed up the walkway to Naomi's door, and

Cahill rang the bell. Pru could hear music coming from inside. The techno beat was so loud she wasn't sure anyone would be able to hear the bell, let alone a knock, but after a few moments, a woman drew back the door and peered out.

Naomi Willis was a pretty brunette who appeared to be several years younger than her brother—early twenties to his early thirties. She was around Pru's height, five-six or so, with a trim, toned body that complemented the pink velour tracksuit she wore.

"Yes?"

Cahill held out his identification, "We're with the FBI," he said. "We'd like to ask you a few questions."

"About what?" she asked warily.

"Your brother. May we come in?"

Alarm flickered in her eyes. "Johnny? What about him? Is he okay?"

"So far as we know, he's fine. We just need to ask you a few questions." Cahill placed his hand on the door. "May we come in?"

Reluctantly, she stepped back, and as they entered, Pru automatically surveyed her surroundings. The living area was to the right of a long, narrow foyer, and the stairway was to the left. Sunlight streamed in through long windows that faced the street, and as the rays bounced off a crystal wind chime, tiny rainbows danced in the air.

The floors were laid with a cool gray slate, but the furnishings were in warmer tones, the fabrics soft and luxurious. The arched doorways and stucco walls gave the town house a Mediterranean feel. It was the kind of place Pru would like to have someday, but would probably never be able to afford.

Naomi hurried across the room and turned off the music. Her sound system looked state-of-the-art, as did the large plasma-screen TV that dominated one wall.

She turned back to face them. "Sorry. I was just going over a new routine," she murmured, running her hands down the sides of her tracksuit.

"You're a dancer?" Pru couldn't help but notice the woman's body. The velour pants rode low on her hips, while the top hit her just above her pierced belly button.

"Fitness instructor," she said.

That would explain the washboard abs, Pru thought a bit enviously. It didn't, however, account for the luxurious surroundings. Since when could fitness instructors afford a place like this?

"You said you had questions about my brother," she said nervously. She motioned to the plush sofa behind them. "Have a seat."

The moment Pru sat on the couch, a huge, white Persian leaped from nowhere onto her lap. It was so unexpected that Pru jumped noticeably, but the supersize feline merely yawned and settled in.

"That's Chester," Naomi said, laughing. "Just shove his big butt off if you don't like cats."

"No, it's okay. I like cats," Pru murmured. Out of the corner of her eye, she saw Cahill grin. She decided any momentary discomfort on her part was worth it to get a reaction like that from him.

Oddly enough, Chester seemed to break the tension in the room. Naomi sat down and slid her hands between her knees. "Actually, Johnny is my stepbrother. But then, being the FBI, you probably already knew that, right?"

Amazing how many people thought the FBI was all-knowing, all-seeing, all-powerful. If only, Pru thought as she ran a tentative hand along Chester's back. He started to purr.

Taking their silence as assent, Naomi nodded. "Yeah, my mother married his father when I was fifteen. It didn't last long. A year, I think, before my old lady got pissed about something and we moved out. But Johnny used to come around sometimes, and even though he was older, we hit it off." Her eyes glowed as she talked about Stiles. She'd been reluctant to let them in, but now she seemed to relish the opportunity to gush over him.

"He wasn't like anyone I ever knew. For sure not like the boys I dated in school. He was smart and funny and sophisticated…" She trailed off. The glow in her eyes turned feverish as she said fiercely, "He didn't do it, you know. He didn't kill those women. He's innocent, and we're going to prove it."

"How?" Cahill asked.

She lifted her chin. "We have a new attorney, and he's not like that idiot we had before. I could have put on a better defense. The whole trial was nothing but a joke. The prosecution didn't even have a case, and yet Johnny's attorney just sat there like some moron and refused to object while they paraded one lame witness after another to the stand. It never should have gotten that far. Anyone with half a brain could see that the charges were trumped up because the cops were under a lot of pressure to make an arrest. So they pinned those murders on Johnny."

Well, well, Pru thought. That was some performance. Naomi Willis had been well coached. Or brainwashed.

"Is that what Stiles told you?" Cahill asked.

Naomi's eyes flashed with anger. "He didn't have to tell me. I was there. I sat through the whole trial, and then I watched them lead Johnny away in handcuffs. The way they treated him was horrible. He was mortified." She drew a long breath. "But it won't be for much longer. He'll be out soon, and then we'll show them. We'll show them all."

"Show who?" Cahill pressed.

The woman shrugged. "The jury. His attorney. Everyone. Like I said, he's innocent and we're going to prove it."

"You seem pretty sure of that."

Her smile was cagey. "Oh, I am. You wait and see."

She seemed to catch herself then, and she looked

almost contrite. "But that's not why you're here, is it? You said you had questions?"

Cahill reached into his jacket pocket and brought out the pictures of the victims they'd tried to show Stiles the day before. He handed them to Naomi. "I'd like you to take a look at these photographs and tell me if you recognize any of these women."

Reluctantly, she accepted the pictures and studied them one by one, pausing to frown over Clare's. "I've seen her before."

Pru and Cahill exchanged a glance. "Do you know where?"

She put a finger to her chin as she gazed down at the picture. Then she shrugged. "Maybe at a club, but I'm not sure."

"A nightclub, you mean?"

She shrugged again.

"Which nightclub? Take your time," Pru urged. "This is important."

"I don't know," she said stubbornly. "I go to a lot of clubs, and I'm not even sure that's where I saw her."

"But you do recognize her?"

"I thought I did, but now I'm not so sure. I'm no good with faces."

"But you—"

Cahill shot Pru a warning look, and she immediately backed off. His message was loud and clear. She was pressing too hard.

Taking a tissue from her pocket, she dabbed at her

eye. "I think I have something in my eye," she murmured.

"It's probably a cat hair," Naomi said. "Happens to me all the time."

"Do you mind if I use your powder room?" Pru lifted the heavy cat off her lap and put him on the floor. "I need a mirror."

"I guess that'd be okay. It's just off the foyer by the stairs," Naomi said, although she didn't seem too keen on the idea. She turned to watch as Pru left the room.

Pru could hear the rumble of Cahill's voice as he drew the young woman's attention, but she couldn't tell what he said.

Scouting out the powder room, Pru turned on the light and closed the door. Then after a few seconds, she peered out. She could still hear their voices, but she couldn't see them from the foyer, nor they her.

Another room was located at the end of the hallway, just beyond the stairs. The door stood open, and Pru could see that the space was a bedroom. Glancing over her shoulder, she stole down the hallway and peeked inside.

The room was so spacious Pru assumed it was the master suite. A wall of arched windows opened onto a courtyard, and a king-size bed with a leather headboard occupied an adjoining wall. Directly opposite the bed was a fireplace, and on the wall over the mantle hung another plasma-screen TV.

As impressive as the individual accoutrements

were, however, none was the focal point. That honor went to the shrine that had been erected in one corner of the room.

It consisted of a low wooden table covered with votive candles, a kneeling pillow and a framed picture that hung on the wall above the table.

Glancing over her shoulder again, Pru slipped inside and tiptoed across the room. Her gaze went immediately to the photograph, and her heart jumped in recognition.

It was a picture of John Allen Stiles.

CAHILL STILL SEEMED preoccupied after they left the town house, and Pru couldn't help wondering why. Of course, the shrine she'd found in Naomi Willis's bedroom was enough to worry anyone, but Pru had a feeling that whatever Cahill had on his mind was something of a more personal nature.

Once again, she found herself thinking about everything her father had told her the evening before. Cahill's daughter had been attacked and he blamed himself. It was a normal reaction for any father but, considering Cahill's profession, his guilt would cut even more deeply.

An FBI agent who had apprehended some of the most violent criminals in the country couldn't protect his own daughter...it must have nearly killed him.

Pru's heart went out to him, but there was nothing she could do. It was obvious he didn't want to talk about whatever was bothering him, and they didn't know one another well enough for her to force the issue.

His mood, however, didn't improve as the day wore on, and when they returned to the office late that afternoon, he asked Pru to set up a short meeting with Tim Sessions. While they waited for Tim to arrive, Cahill stood silently at the window and stared out at the falling twilight. He didn't turn when Tim entered the office a few minutes later, nor did he acknowledge the younger agent in any way. He appeared so lost in thought that Pru wondered if he was even aware of their presence.

Tim gave her a questioning look, but Pru merely shrugged. She had no idea what was going on inside the man's head.

"I've got the information you requested," Tim finally said. Taking the chair next to Pru's, he placed his laptop on Cahill's desk and opened the lid. "TheForgottenMan.com is run by a Canadian activist group called the Coalition for Fair and Humane Treatment of Prisoners, and it appears to be one of the largest purveyors of Web space to inmates on the Internet. They deal primarily with men on death row, but they also have lifers like Stiles. They offer ads free of charge to prisoners here in the U.S., enabling them to reach millions of potential sympathizers worldwide. The inmates use the ads for everything from soliciting pro bono attorneys to pleading for letters to help fill their lonely hours."

"Stiles already has a pro bono attorney," Pru said. "Sid Zellman said that a friend of the court had referred him to their firm."

Tim grimaced. "Yes, well, judging by Stiles's ad, I don't think legal advice is what he's looking for."

"Meaning?"

"See for yourself." Tim loaded the site, then scrolled down an alphabetical directory to click on Stiles's link. When the page opened, Pru caught her breath.

The picture of John Allen Stiles was identical to the one she'd seen in Naomi Willis's bedroom. If the graphic had been displayed on any other Web site, no one would ever have guessed that such a pleasant-looking man was a convicted criminal, much less one who was currently serving consecutive life sentences for the brutal slaying of five young women.

To the naive eye, he would simply appear to be an attractive man in his early thirties with a gentle smile and a relaxed demeanor.

His eyes gave him away, though. They were dark, cold, soulless. And terrifyingly seductive.

He was dressed in street clothes, his hair trimmed and styled, his nails perfectly groomed. He held a large white cat in his arms, and the caption over the photograph read: *Animal lover seeks warm and caring heart to bring a ray of sunshine into a cold and lonely existence.*

Cahill left the window and walked across the room to study the picture over Pru's shoulder.

"It's the same photograph I saw hanging in Naomi Willis's bedroom," she told him.

"Looks like the same cat we saw there, too."

"I thought the kitty was a masterful stroke." Tim's tone sounded almost admiring. "You've got to hand it to these guys. They really know how to work the system. They put up an innocuous picture like that, and the women who are sucked in don't have a clue how dangerous they are. I mean, some of these inmates are so vicious they have to be tied facedown to a gurney during visits with their own lawyers."

Pru suppressed a shudder. "Can you imagine how a victim's family would feel if they ran across a picture like that?"

"Yes, actually, I can," Cahill muttered.

Pru bit her lip. "Do you still think Stiles could be using this Web site to solicit photographs of potential victims?"

Cahill shrugged. "It makes a lot of sense when you think about it. The ad probably generates dozens, if not hundreds of letters from women who monitor these kinds of sites. A lot of them undoubtedly send in photographs, and all Stiles has to do is pick the one that matches his criteria...his fantasy, if you will, and then he gives the picture to his surrogate, along with the woman's address. She probably spills her guts to him in her letters so that the surrogate is armed with enough personal information to make a connection with her."

Pru frowned. "Sounds like the way Max Tripp's P.I. firm operates." She turned to Tim. "Were you able to find out anything about Tripp Investigations?"

Tim logged off and closed his laptop. "First of all, the agency has two separate divisions that act independently of one another. Tripp Investigations handles routine cases like nanny surveillance, cheating spouses, insurance fraud, hidden assets, things like that. The other division is internally referred to as Matchmakers Underground, and their specialty is 'designing coincidences.' They deal exclusively with wealthy male clients who are willing to pay the big bucks for an opportunity to meet the woman of their dreams."

Pru already knew all that. "What about Danny Costello?"

Tim nodded. "He's an ex-cop, just like you said. He was fired a few years back for using unnecessary force on a suspect. The charges were eventually dropped, but the department felt he was too much of a liability to keep him around so they found another reason to get rid of him. The guy has a real temper, from what I hear."

"And Tripp hired him anyway?"

"Like I said, the charges were dropped, and a man's innocent until proven guilty. But get this." Tim's eyes glittered with excitement. "His old partner was none other than Janet Stryker. My contact at HPD told me that Costello was a real hotshot back then, always getting citations, his name in the news and so forth. Stryker got herself partnered with him, and they made quite a team for a while. Then things got a little too hot and steamy between them, and Stryker's husband walked out on her. He was a cop, too, and, according to my source, he raised a nasty stink about the affair. Somehow, though, Stryker managed to come out of the mess looking like a victim. She made noises about sexual harassment, and it was the kiss of death for Costello's career. A few months later, she was promoted to detective and never looked back."

The story supported Pru's initial assessment of Janet Stryker. The woman was manipulative, ambitious and cold-blooded. It also made sense why she'd been reluctant to follow up on a lead involving Danny Costello. An ex-partner who was also an ex-lover might know things that could derail a promising career.

"Funny thing about Costello," Tim said. "I tried to dig up a photograph, but pictures of the guy seem to be in short supply. I haven't been able to find an address for him, either."

"Then we need to talk to Janet Stryker," Pru said.

"Absolutely not." Cahill gave her a scowling reprimand as he walked around the desk and sat down. His frigid eyes berated first Pru, then Tim. "We don't deal with gossip in this office. We work with facts. I suggest you both remember that."

"Uh, sorry," Tim muttered. "The information seemed relevant to me."

"It *is* relevant," Pru insisted, wondering if she was about to torpedo her own career. "Janet Stryker's past relationship with Danny Costello could explain why she hasn't gone after his connection to Clare McDonald."

"That's pure speculation," Cahill accused.

Pru drew a breath. "With all due respect, sir, I disagree. Tim's right. The information is relevant, and we need to aggressively pursue this angle."

"With all due respect, Agent Dunlop," Cahill said in a tight, humorless voice, "I'm telling you to back off."

"But, sir—"

He gave her a look that warned she was treading on thin ice. Pru didn't understand his attitude. It almost seemed as if he was trying to protect Janet Stryker, but why would he? He'd given Pru the impression that he'd only met the woman once or twice.

Besides, Cahill wasn't the type to let his personal feelings interfere with an investigation. Something else was going on here.

Tim stood and gathered up his laptop. "I'll let you know what else I find out."

Pru rose, too, and followed Tim to the door. But at the last moment, she turned and came back over to Cahill's desk.

He glanced up. "Yes?"

She hesitated as her heart started to respond to the

way he looked at her. Those eyes…would she ever get used to their impact? "This is none of my business, but…are you okay?"

His brow furrowed. "I told you this morning, I'm fine. I suggest you let the matter drop."

"I'm sorry. It's just…the information Tim found—"

"What about it?"

"It's a good lead. We can't just ignore it," she said stubbornly. "Sir, you have a theory that Stiles is using the Internet to scout out his victims. But I have a different theory. Just hear me out for a minute." She rushed on before he could stop her. "Think about what they do at Tripp Investigations. They follow these women. They talk to their friends, family and business associates so that they can gain the kind of insight that will allow their clients to form instant bonds with them. What if someone else is using that information, too?"

"The killer, you mean."

"Or his surrogate. That would explain why someone like Clare McDonald could have been so vulnerable to him. He knew things about her, intimate things, and he used that information to establish a relationship with her. To make her fall in love with him." Pru straightened. "And the way I see it, he'd have to be someone on the inside." Which brought them back to Danny Costello. And Janet Stryker.

"Not necessarily," Cahill said. "Anyone with technical expertise could hack into the company's system and access their files. He could have transferred the information onto his own computer to use as he needed it."

"So you agree with me, then," she said almost triumphantly. "This is a lead we need to pursue. And I think we should start with Janet Stryker."

Cahill sat back in his chair and gazed up at her, his eyes going so stark they made Pru shiver. Then slowly he rose and came around the desk to face her. "One thing you'd better get straight pretty damn fast, Agent Dunlop. This is my team, and I call the shots."

Pru swallowed. "Yes, sir. I didn't mean to—"

"Janet Stryker is off-limits to you," he cut in coldly. "Is that clear?"

Crystal clear, Pru thought with a sinking heart.

Chapter Nine

Pru slid into the chair across the table from Tiffany that night and gave her a tentative smile. Considering the cold shoulder she'd received at Clare's funeral, Pru wasn't at all certain of her reception. But to her surprise, Tiffany returned her smile.

Pru tried not to appear surprised by her reaction. "Thanks for agreeing to meet me."

"No problem. I'm glad to see you," Tiffany said.

She was?

Wow, Pru thought as she got her first good look at the woman. Not only had Tiffany's attitude changed, but she looked terrific. The gaunt, strained mask that had been so prevalent at Clare's funeral had vanished, and now she appeared more like the old Tiffany, except better. Her eyes sparkled, her skin glowed. She looked radiant.

So what was up with that? Pru wondered.

She'd asked Tiffany to meet her in the same bar

where they'd had drinks on the night of Clare's murder, hoping the familiarity of the place might jar Tiffany's memory. It was possible Clare had let something slip that Tiffany had forgotten. Pru realized she was grasping at straws, but she figured it was worth a shot.

She'd wanted to talk to Tiffany days ago, but the poor woman had been such a mess at Clare's funeral that Pru had been reluctant to intrude upon her grief. The service hadn't been the time or place to question her, but with each passing day, the surrogate could be getting closer and closer to his next victim. Pru couldn't wait any longer.

The same waiter who'd served them the first night came over to take their orders. "Hey, I remember you two. Welcome back." He flashed Tiffany his killer smile. "Don't tell me…apple martini, right?"

Tiffany shifted her blond hair over one shoulder, then smiled up at him. "You have a good memory." Her gaze dropped. "Among other things."

The waiter looked a little flustered by her flattery, and Pru supposed she couldn't blame him. Tiffany hadn't given him the time of day the last time they'd been in. Pru couldn't help wondering again about the sudden changes in the woman.

Reluctantly, the waiter turned to Pru. "And for you—"

"A Diet Coke," she supplied before he had time to struggle.

He looked wounded. "I was just about to say that."

"Sorry."

"No problem." He grinned. "I'll have your drinks right out. Enjoy your evening, ladies."

As Pru watched him hurry away, her attention was caught by a man seated at the end of the bar. Their gazes locked for one split second and, with a shock, she realized he was the same man who had been checking her out that first night.

"Déjà vu," she muttered.

"What? Oh, the waiter you mean." Tiffany glanced over her shoulder. "I remember him, too."

"What about that guy at the end of the bar?" Pru nodded in the man's direction. "He just came in. Have you ever seen him before?"

Tiffany expertly canvassed the bar, but the man had swiveled so that all she could see was the back of his head. She turned to Pru with a shrug. "I don't know. Why?"

"He was here the last time we were in."

Tiffany glanced at him again, but he still had his back to her. "I can't really tell. Anyway," she said, as the waiter placed their drinks in front of them, "I was glad to hear from you, Pru. I've been meaning to call you." Tiffany bit her lip. "I'm sorry for the way I behaved at Clare's funeral. I was just so upset…"

"You don't have to apologize. You two were always so close. I can't imagine how hard this must be for you."

Tiffany blinked back sudden tears. "It is. You have no idea."

"How are you holding up?" Pru asked sympathetically.

"Each day gets a little easier, I guess. But sometimes I still can't believe she's really gone. I find myself picking up the phone to call her and tell her about something that happened at work. Or about a new outfit I bought. A movie I went to see. A trip I want to take." Tiffany sighed. "Everyone says it'll take time."

"I'm sure that's true. But in the meantime, if there's anything I can do…"

Tiffany glanced up, her eyes still bright. "Do you mean that?"

"Of course," Pru said. "Just name it."

"There is one thing…" Tiffany trailed off, as if reluctant to voice the favor she wanted to ask.

Pru tried to hide her wariness. "What is it?"

Tiffany ran a fingertip around the rim of her glass. "The police have released Clare's town house. I promised her folks I'd go over there tomorrow and pack up some of her things, but…I can't face that place alone. Is there any chance you could meet me there?" she asked hopefully.

Even though the next day was Saturday, Pru had planned to work. But she could take off a few hours, and besides, she wouldn't mind having a look around Clare's home.

"What time do you want to meet?"

Relief flooded Tiffany's eyes. "Really? You'll do it?"

"Of course. Just tell me when."

Tiffany thought for a moment. "I have a few things I need to do first, but I should be able to get there around ten. Is that all right?"

"Ten it is."

Tiffany let out a long breath. "Oh, God, Pru, you don't know how grateful I am. There's just no way I could do that alone."

"It's okay. I'm happy to help out."

Tiffany glanced at her watch. "I hate to do this to you, but I really can't stay. I…have plans." She looked a little sheepish as her gaze darted away.

Pru still couldn't get over the changes in Tiffany. Outwardly, she appeared to have bounced back since Clare's funeral. She had color in her cheeks and that strange sparkle in her eyes. It made Pru wonder about the nature of her plans.

"I'll try to make this quick," she said as she shoved aside her drink. "I want you to tell me everything Clare said about the guy she was seeing. I don't care how insignificant it may seem, I need to know everything you can remember." When Tiffany started to protest, Pru said, "I know this is painful, but it's important."

"You didn't think it was so important when we were here before," Tiffany blurted.

Her bitterness caught Pru off guard. Only a moment earlier, she'd seemed so warm and friendly. Had that been an act?

Pru sat back in her chair. "I'm sorry I didn't take your concerns more seriously."

Tiffany's eyes glinted with anger before she glanced away. Then taking a deep, shuddering breath, she appeared to force her emotions aside. "It's not your fault. Deep down, I know that. Even if you had taken me seriously, it wouldn't have done any good. The police said Clare was killed later that same night. Have you thought about that, Pru?" She leaned forward, her eyes shadowed with grief and guilt. "While we sat here having drinks, he was planning to kill her. It makes me sick when I think about it."

"I know. But what we have to concentrate on now is stopping him before he can do it again. That's why I need your help, Tiff. If you can think of anything she might have said about him, anything at all, it could be a big help to us."

Tiffany smoothed back a strand of blond hair. "I told you. Clare wouldn't tell me anything about him."

"Did she ever call him anything…a nickname, maybe?"

Tiffany shook her head.

"Did she mention what kind of car he drove?"

"No! I don't know anything!"

Pru sighed. "Did she ever say how they met? Could it have been over the Internet?"

Tiffany's gaze lifted. "You mean…like an online dating service?"

"Maybe. Did she ever mention anything like that?"

"I don't think so."

"What about a pen pal?"

"A pen pal?" Tiffany looked startled. "I don't know…it doesn't sound like Clare—" She broke off, her gaze going past Pru's shoulder.

"What?" Pru pressed. "Did you remember something?"

"I think I see someone I know," she said in a strange voice.

Pru started to turn. "The guy that was at the bar?"

"No. That woman over there. She's sitting at the table in the corner." Tiffany gave a slight nod.

Pru turned to inspect the tables behind them.

"See the brunette in the red dress? I've seen her somewhere before."

At that moment, Pru's gaze landed on the woman Tiffany had spotted through the crowd. The red dress drew her attention first and then, as the woman pivoted in her chair, Pru caught her breath. It was Janet Stryker.

She looked different tonight. On the two previous occasions when Pru had met her, she'd been dressed in jeans and a snug-fitting blazer—a practical yet hip uniform for an up-and-coming detective.

Tonight, however, she'd pulled out all the stops. Even though she was seated, the cut and fabric of her dress left little to the imagination.

Her dark hair fell to her shoulders, and the subtle layers sexily framed her oval face. Pru had virtually the same cut, but most days she pulled her hair back and clipped it up, letting strands fall haphazardly from the clasp. The style was quick and practical, but not all that flattering.

Suddenly, Pru was all too aware of how she looked tonight with her hair all straggly, her makeup worn away, and her clothing—dark pin-striped trousers and a white cotton blouse—rumpled from a long day at work.

She turned back to Tiffany, whose own simple black dress was nothing short of stunning. "Her name is Janet Stryker. She's an HPD homicide detective. You probably talked to her after Clare's death."

Tiffany shook her head. "No, I didn't. The detective who interviewed me was male. All male," she murmured, sounding more like the old Tiffany with each passing moment.

Yes, a cop would definitely appeal to Tiffany, at least for a while. "Well, then you probably saw Sgt. Stryker at the station when you went in to give your statement."

She shook her head. "I gave my statement to Sgt. Reed. That's not where I saw her." Tiffany scowled as her gaze lingered on Janet Stryker. Then she snapped her fingers. "Wait a minute. I know where I saw her, and it didn't have anything to do with her being a cop."

"Where did you see her?" Pru asked anxiously.

"It was at this club that Clare and I used to go to.

A place called Acceleration. It's on Montrose, a few blocks from Clare's town house."

Pru's tone sharpened. "Did you and Clare go there often?"

Tiffany shrugged. "A few times, I guess. Why?"

"Did you tell the police about this club?"

"No. I'd forgotten all about it until just now when I saw that woman. She had the same dress on that night at the club. I remember, because Clare has…had one just like it."

Pru dug in her purse for the photographs of the other two victims. Handing them to Tiffany, she said, "Do you remember seeing either of these women at the club?"

Tiffany took the pictures and studied them for a moment. Her gaze kept going back to the first victim, Ellie Markham, then she shook her head. "I don't know. It's possible."

"Take another look," Pru urged. "This is important."

"I may have seen them, but I can't be sure. It's dark and smoky inside the club and half the women who go there look like this." Tiffany glanced up. "You don't think that's where the killer saw Clare, do you?"

Pru didn't answer. "Do you remember if she talked to any strange men that night?"

Tiffany lifted a brow. "Of course, she did. That's kind of the point of going to a place like that."

"Anyone stick out in your mind? Someone who might have acted overly persistent?"

"Not that I recall."

"Did she leave with anyone?"

Tiffany gave her a reproachful look. "Clare wasn't the type to pick up strange men in clubs. We went there to party and dance and have a good time, but that was the extent of it."

"Would she have given her phone number to someone she met there?"

"No, never. Clare was very cautious about that sort of thing..." Tiffany seemed to catch herself. "At least, I thought she was." Her gaze moved back to Janet Stryker. "Speaking of picking up guys," she murmured. "I wonder who he is."

"He who?"

"That man with Janet Stryker." Tiffany gave him a quick assessment. "Not bad, but he looks a little intense for my taste."

Pru turned again. Janet Stryker had been alone earlier, but now a man was seated across the table from her. When Pru saw who he was, her heart nearly catapulted out of her chest.

The man with Janet Stryker was John Cahill.

A LITTLE WHILE LATER, Pru hurried across the darkened parking lot to her car. She'd been so taken aback by seeing Cahill with Janet Stryker that she'd barely said goodbye when Tiffany got up to leave. Pru had insisted on picking up the tab since the meeting had been her idea, but she'd hung around only long enough to hastily scrawl her name across the credit card receipt before bolting for the door.

She had no idea why she was upset, or why she'd been so hell-bent on getting out of that place before Cahill spotted her. Why hadn't she just gone over to say hello? What would have been the harm in that?

Instead, she'd behaved like a schoolgirl with her first serious crush.

Pru berated herself all the way to her car. How was she going to forge a working relationship with Cahill if she kept acting like such an idiot?

She was way too old for this kind of behavior. If she wasn't careful, he would pick up on her feelings for him, and then she'd be forced to transfer out of SKURRT. Pru's career, along with her pride, would be left in tatters.

Her father was right. She had to find a way to get Cahill out of her system, but at the moment, she didn't have a clue how to do that.

What on earth did he see in Janet Stryker anyway? Okay, so she was attractive and sexy. But she was also an arrogant, manipulative bi—

Careful, Pru cautioned herself. She was fast losing her objectivity here, and if there was anything she'd always prided herself on, it was her professional detachment from her cases.

She would approach Janet Stryker just as she would any other suspect, even if it killed her.

Wait a minute.

Pru slowed her steps. Since when had she started thinking of Janet Stryker as a suspect? When she'd learned Stryker had once been Danny Costello's partner? Or when she'd seen her with John Cahill?

Pru thought about the club Tiffany had mentioned earlier. Could that be yet another lead? Another connection to Janet Stryker?

Pru was almost to her car when she became aware of footsteps behind her. Someone was following her.

Her pulse quickened as she pretended to reach for her keys in her shoulder bag. She gripped the handle of her gun, and when the footsteps closed in on her, she spun.

The sight of her weapon caught her would-be assailant completely by surprise, and he stumbled backward. Raising his hands over his head, he stuttered in alarm, "Whoa...d-don't shoot or anything. I didn't mean to scare you."

Pru recognized him at once. He was the man who had been checking her out at the end of the bar. "Why are you following me?" she demanded.

He still had his hands in the air, but now that she had a closer look at him, he didn't seem all that frightened. Quite the opposite, in fact. His expression mocked her. "I want to talk to you," he said.

"About what?"

His voice lowered conspiratorially. "I know who you are, Agent Dunlop."

Pru's hand tightened on her weapon. "You have me

at a disadvantage," she said with a frown. "Who the hell are you?"

"Danny Costello."

The name shot through her with the punch of a bullet, but she tried not to show her alarm. "Let's see some ID."

He lowered his hands and lazily reached for his wallet. Flipping it open, he handed it to her.

He had a Texas driver's license along with his P.I. license. Pru closed the wallet and tossed it back to him. "You said you wanted to talk. I'm listening."

"Actually..." His dark head was slightly bent, and the way he gazed up at her made her blood run cold. He'd seemed like an ordinary guy in the bar, but now, alone with him in the dark, Pru thought he looked sinister. "I hear you want to talk to me."

She kept her voice even. "Who told you that, Mr. Costello?"

"Danny." He sounded menacing even when he smiled. "You haven't exactly been subtle, Agent Dunlop. You were the one who gave my name to the police as a possible suspect in the Clare McDonald murder case. Of course, you had no idea then that you'd be the one who could also give me an alibi, did you?"

"What are you talking about?"

His expression altered subtly. "I was here the night Clare McDonald was murdered. You saw me."

"That was early in the evening," Pru said, trying to ignore the shivers racing up and down her back. "I have no idea what you did after you left here. And come to think of it," she said slowly, her finger still on the trigger, "why were you here that night?"

"I followed your friend," he said candidly. "The blonde. Tiffany Beaumont. I had a few more questions I needed to ask her."

"About Clare?"

He shrugged.

"You were wasting your time," Pru said. "Tiffany was on to you. That's why she wanted me to meet her here. She already knew that you weren't who you said you were."

"I screwed up," he said with another shrug. "So sue me."

Pru wasn't fooled by his flip tone. He wanted something. "So how did you happen to pick Todd Hollister's name, anyway? What did you do? Go through Clare's yearbook?"

"As a matter of fact, I did. I'd like to say your senior picture doesn't do you justice, Agent Dunlop, but you were quite a looker back then. You still would be if you weren't trying so hard not to be."

"Whether you find me attractive or not is immaterial," she said.

"Really? That's not the message you sent in the bar." His tone continued to mock her.

Pru decided not to rise to his bait. "Who else besides Tiffany did you contact about Clare?"

"Her neighbors, business associates, old high

school classmates. That's what we do at Tripp Investigations."

"I know all about what you do," Pru said coolly. "Who hired you to follow Clare? Who saw her as the woman of his dreams?"

"My, my, you've been a busy girl," he said with that same sinister smile.

"Who's your client, Mr. Costello?"

"I can't tell you that. I signed a confidentiality agreement not to divulge the identity of any of our clients."

"We could subpoena your records," Pru threatened.

He laughed. "Go right ahead. It's not my company, so why should I care? But you know as well as I do that by the time you find a judge willing to sign the order, you could have another dead woman on your hands."

It was all Pru could do not to react. "You sound as if you know something about this case."

"I know what you're dealing with," he said.

"And just what are we dealing with, Mr. Costello?"

"Let's start with what you're not dealing with." He moved toward her in the darkness. Pru had to fight the urge to back away from him. "You've got it all wrong, Agent Dunlop. I didn't have anything to do with any of those murders."

She lifted a brow. "And I'm supposed to take your word for that?"

"Like I said, if you want to waste time pursuing a

dead-end lead, you could wind up with another body on your hands."

"Mr. Costello, if you know something about these murders—"

"I saw the killer, Agent Dunlop."

Pru caught her breath. "Where?"

"I had Clare McDonald under surveillance, remember? I saw her with the killer."

"Then why haven't you gone to the police?" Pru demanded.

"Because, thanks to you, the police seem a little too interested in my whereabouts that night, and I have no intention of becoming a patsy for HPD Homicide. So in my own self-interest, I've decided to lay low for a while. You should be flattered," he murmured. "The only thing that drew me out of hiding was the prospect of talking to you."

Pru wasn't flattered. She was still scared to death and not at all convinced that the man wasn't trying to cover his own ass. "You said you saw the killer with Clare. Who is he?"

"I can't give you a name."

"Can't or won't?"

He shrugged.

"What about a description?"

"Sorry."

"Mr. Costello—"

He moved very quickly and before Pru could stop him, he was standing so near she could feel his breath

on her face as he wove his fingers through her hair.
She still had her weapon drawn, but it didn't seem to
faze him.

"Stand back," she ordered.

His fingers tightened in her hair as he lowered
his voice. "Do you want to find the killer, Agent
Dunlop?"

She lifted her chin and gazed into his eyes. They
were very dark. Almost as dark as Cahill's. Slowly she
nodded.

He put his lips very close to her ear. "Then stop
thinking like a profiler and start acting like a cop.
Stop trying to analyze the killer. You'll only end up
running in circles. Go back to the basics. Look for
méans, motive and opportunity."

"The motive of a serial killer is not always deter-
minable."

"There you go again." His tone castigated her.
"Still thinking like a profiler. Who said anything about
a serial killer?"

"The MO, the staging of the crime scene, the posing of the bodies…they're identical in all three cases.
That can't be a coincidence."

"I never said it was." Releasing her, he moved back
a step or two. Pru hadn't even realized she'd been
holding her breath until it came out in a rush.

"Ask yourself one question, Agent Dunlop. Who
would benefit from these deaths?"

"Benefit?" She stared at him in confusion. "That

would imply a connection between the victims. There isn't one."

"You just haven't found it yet. Start with the places where their paths would most likely have crossed. They lived in the same neighborhood, so check the grocery stores, beauty salons…a local nightclub."

Pru's tone sharpened. "A nightclub?"

He said nothing.

"You know more than you're telling me," she accused.

"You're a smart agent. You'll figure it out. A case like this could make or break an ambitious woman's career," he said softly. "But I'm sure that's already occurred to you, hasn't it?"

His words reminded her of something Cahill had said to her the day he'd approved her transfer when she'd wondered why Janet Stryker had been so uncooperative.

Put yourself in her place. She's an ambitious detective who's just caught a big case. It wouldn't do her career any good to have the FBI come in and steal her thunder.

And then earlier, in Cahill's office, Tim Sessions had told them what he'd dug up on Costello. He'd been a hotshot cop until he'd become embroiled with Janet Stryker. She'd used him, then hung him out to dry when he no longer suited her purposes.

"Why are you telling me all this?" she asked Costello. "Why are you willing to help me?"

"Because someone's going to break this case wide open, and I'd like it to be you."

"Why?"

"There's an old saying, Agent Dunlop. Payback's hell."

Then he turned and walked off without another word.

"Agent Dunlop? Are you okay?"

At the sound of Cahill's voice, Pru spun. She'd been so engrossed in rehashing her conversation with Costello that she hadn't heard him approach.

But now that she knew he was so near, her heart started to pound. She couldn't help herself. He always had that effect on her.

Plus, she was still unnerved by her confrontation with Danny Costello. She hadn't put away her weapon until he was out of sight, and only then had she realized how badly her hands were trembling.

She was still trembling, and she hoped Cahill wouldn't notice.

She gazed at him in the darkness. Even though she couldn't see his face clearly, she knew that his expression would be serious. Intense. She wondered suddenly how all that intensity would play out in the bedroom.

"Agent Dunlop?"

"I'm, uh, okay," she stuttered. "I just had a run-in with Danny Costello."

"Costello?" Cahill took a step toward her as his gazed searched the parking lot. "What did he want?"

"He said he wanted to talk to me."

"About what?"

Pru drew a breath, trying to steady her nerves. "He somehow found out that I'm the one who gave his name to the police. He wanted me to know that I'm chasing a dead-end lead."

"He would say that, wouldn't he?" Cahill's attention came back to her. "You look a little shaky. He didn't threaten you, did he?"

"No, he didn't threaten me." Far from offending her, the protective note in Cahill's voice sent a thrill of awareness coursing through Pru. She could take care of herself, but it never hurt to have someone watching your back. Especially when that someone was John Cahill.

"What else did he say?"

"He—" She broke off. Costello hadn't really said anything specific, but Pru had gotten the distinct impression that he'd been trying to send her a message. And that message somehow involved Janet Stryker.

Considering Cahill's defense of the detective earlier and now his appearance with her tonight, Pru wasn't at all certain she wanted to even bring up Stryker's name. Besides, she needed time to digest the implications of her conversation with Costello. It was possible she'd read him entirely wrong. Then again, maybe she hadn't.

"We can discuss it tomorrow at the office," she said. "Right now, I should probably let you get back inside."

"I was just leaving."

Alone? she wondered. Or was Janet Stryker waiting for him in the car? The notion made Pru slightly nauseous. "Then don't let me keep you."

He looked at her strangely, as if detecting a note in her voice that shouldn't have been there. "I was going to grab something to eat before heading home," he said. "Have you had dinner?"

The question caught Pru so off guard, it took her a moment to answer. "Uh, no."

"Are you hungry?"

She hadn't been until that very moment, but now she found that she was ravenous. "Yeah, I guess I am."

He tilted his head, gazing down at her. "You like omelets?"

"Sure…who doesn't?"

"Then follow me, Agent. I know a place that makes the best western omelets you've ever tasted."

His sudden smile stunned Pru. Knocked her socks off. Made him look ten years younger and a million times sexier, and that was saying something.

Pru had a feeling that another smile like that, and she just might be willing to follow him anywhere.

Chapter Ten

Half an hour later, Pru found herself seated at the bar in Cahill's apartment, watching him chop and sauté vegetables, heat the omelet pan and make fresh salsa in the blender. For someone who had only been a bachelor for little more than a year, he certainly seemed to know his way around the kitchen.

Pru could hardly believe that she was actually sitting in the man's apartment while he prepared dinner for her. Two days ago, he hadn't even recognized her in the elevator. At least, that was the impression he'd given. And now here she was. Here *he* was.

Her sudden reversal of fortune was nothing short of amazing, Pru decided. If someone had told her five years ago that she would someday be working with the great John Cahill, she would never have believed him.

But they were not only working together, they were about to enjoy dinner together…just the two of them…alone in Cahill's apartment.

She tried not to stare as he moved about the kitchen, but it was difficult not to. He'd taken off his jacket and tie and rolled up his sleeves. His collar was unbuttoned, and Pru could see just enough tanned flesh to remind her of all that glistening skin she'd witnessed at the gym. The man was pushing forty, but aside from the lines around his mouth and eyes, he didn't look it. He was in fantastic shape.

But his body was just one of many things that Pru found so attractive. Everything about him fascinated her. Who he was and what he'd accomplished. He was *John Cahill,* for Pete's sake. Pru had never met anyone half as interesting, and as she covertly studied him—his head bent to his work—she felt the pull she'd being trying so hard to resist for the last two days slowly fight its way to the surface.

She wondered what it would be like to kiss him. To be kissed by him. He had a wonderful mouth. Sexy and sensuous, with just a hint of the cynic in his smile.

He was a serious man in a serious profession, and if he brought even half as much passion to the bedroom as he did to his cases, Pru could only imagine how shattering his lovemaking would be.

But it would probably be better for her if she *didn't* try to imagine.

He looked up at that moment, caught her gaze, and smiled.

And Pru melted.

Crush…infatuation…call it what you liked, she

wanted John Cahill as she'd never wanted any man in her life. He was not someone she would easily get out of her system.

Like a master chef, he flipped the omelets onto heated plates, then brought them over to the bar, along with fresh salsa and steaming cups of coffee.

Pru spooned the salsa onto her omelet as Cahill came around the counter and sat down beside her. "Careful," he warned. "That stuff has a kick."

"I'm a native Texan, so I'm not too worried," she assured him. "Jalapeño peppers are my favorite vegetable."

He lifted one brow. "If you say so."

Pru noticed that rather than start on his own omelet, he watched in amusement while she sampled hers. "Whoa!" She put a hand to her mouth. "You weren't kidding. That's some kick."

He got up and poured her a glass of water. "Too hot?"

"No, perfect," she croaked as she gulped the water. When her mouth finally cooled down, she tried to eat around the salsa. "This is really good. Where did you learn to cook?"

"I wouldn't call that cooking," he said with a shrug. "Omelets are about the only thing I know how to make. I used to whip them up for my daughter and me when I'd get home late from work. She'd wait up, and we'd have dinner together while she told me about her day."

And just where had Mrs. Cahill been during those dinners? Pru wondered. Given the same opportunity, Pru knew where she'd be.

Cahill paused thoughtfully. "I don't think I've made omelets since Jessie left for college."

"You miss her," Pru said.

He picked up his fork. "It's crazy. She's a student at the University of Houston, so she's actually closer to my apartment now than when she lived with her mother in Champions. But it's still…different somehow."

"She's growing up."

"Yeah." He didn't sound too happy about the prospect. "She used to come over a lot on weekends, and we'd rent movies, microwave popcorn, just hang out and relax." He glanced around. "This place seems so quiet now."

"That's why they call it the empty-nest syndrome." Pru sipped her coffee. "My parents went through the same thing when I went off to school. I bet yours did, too."

"Probably." He shrugged again. "I just wish she'd call a little more often. I tried her cell phone earlier and couldn't reach her."

"Well, it is Friday night," Pru gently pointed out.

He grimaced. "I know. And the last thing I want to do is come across as an overbearing, overprotective jerk of a dad who thinks he has to keep tabs on his daughter's whereabouts every minute of the day. But…it's not like her to turn her cell phone off. She

knows her mother and I like to stay in touch with her.
Yet she seems to be going out of her way to cut herself off from us."

Pru studied his profile for a moment. "Are you really that worried about her?"

He turned, and Pru saw the anguish in his eyes even
though he tried to shrug away his concern.

He still feels guilty, she thought. After all this time,
what happened to his daughter was still eating him up
inside.

"I know she's okay," he said. "I've talked to her
roommate, but I can't seem to shake this feeling that
something is wrong."

Pru didn't know what to say to that. He did seem to
be carrying the overprotective father routine to the extreme, but then, everything considered, he had every
right. Pru knew she'd probably be just as concerned.

"I'm sure everything is okay," she murmured.

"You're probably right. I think part of my problem
is that she's just so damn young. And she's been through
so much. I'm not sure she was ready for college."

"Sounds to me as if you're the one who wasn't
ready," Pru said frankly.

His smile turned rueful. "Yeah, it does sound that
way, doesn't it?" His gaze dropped to her now-empty
plate. "So how was the omelet?"

"I think my plate speaks for itself."

He got up to clear away the dishes, and Pru rose
to help.

"No, don't do that," he insisted, taking her plate. "I'll just stack the dishes in the sink and do them later. Go make yourself comfortable, and I'll put on more coffee."

More coffee? Pru was so jittery she was about to start bouncing off the walls, but she wasn't sure the caffeine was entirely to blame.

While Cahill puttered around in the kitchen, Pru wandered into the living room. It was a masculine space, sparsely furnished with a leather sofa and heavy oak tables.

She walked over to the window to admire the view of the downtown skyline. The only thing she could see from her living room window was an oak tree that had somehow survived the construction. A family of squirrels lived in the branches, and she got a kick out of watching them every morning while she had her orange juice.

An easy chair had been placed near the window and positioned so that Cahill could see both the TV and the view in the evenings. A table with a reading lamp and a stack of files was within easy reach. Pru had a similar arrangement in her own apartment.

She picked up a framed photograph from the table and studied it. The girl in the picture was dressed in a royal blue cap and gown with a gold ribbon draped around her shoulders. So his daughter had been an honor student. Somehow, that wasn't surprising.

Turning, Pru held up the picture so that Cahill could see it from the kitchen. "Your daughter?"

His whole face lit up. It was like someone had turned on a light inside him. "Yeah, that's Jessie. Every time I look at that picture, I'm amazed by the passage of time," he said. "It seems like yesterday that she was still in kindergarten."

"My mother said the same thing when I graduated from the academy," Pru said. "I'm not sure she's convinced to this day that I'm actually an FBI agent." She returned the picture and picked up another, this one of Jessie and an elderly man who bore a striking resemblance to Cahill. The pair stood on the deck of a boat in Galveston harbor. Pru recognized the scenery in the background.

"Is this your dad?"

Cahill came out of the kitchen and walked over to her. He took the picture and stared down at it for a moment, a look of sadness flickering across his face. "Yeah. He loved taking Jessie out on that boat. She's a natural sailor, unlike her old man," he said with a grin. "Dad was so proud of her for that. The two of them would go out for hours. I've never seen Jessie so happy as when she's on the water. She's been through a lot for a kid her age, and sometimes I think that boat and my dad helped save her life."

"You talk about him in the past tense," Pru said. "He's gone?"

Cahill nodded. "He died a couple of weeks after that picture was taken. That was the last time he and Jessie were together."

"I'm sorry," Pru said. "It sounds like you and he were really close."

"I guess we were. It was just the two of us when I was growing up, so you learn to depend on one another."

"What about your mother?" Pru asked.

"She died when I was born. Complications after a C-section," he said grimly.

"Oh, my God," Pru said, stricken. She couldn't imagine growing up without her own mother. Her heart went out to Cahill. His daughter wasn't the only one who'd been through a lot.

"I never knew her so I can't really say I suffered from the loss. My dad, though…" He turned and set the picture aside. "I don't think he ever got over it."

"He never remarried?"

"I don't even remember that he dated very much," Cahill said. "I think he was still in love with my mother until the day he died."

"My dad is the same way," Pru said with a pang. "My parents divorced a year ago, but I know he's still crazy about my mother. She's this ultrachic, ultrasophisticated fashion icon who looks just like Grace Kelly. I don't think I've ever seen her without her hair done or her makeup on. And my dad…well, you've seen him."

"He's a good man," Cahill said.

Pru nodded. "The best. They're both wonderful people in their own way, but they couldn't be more different. They're like night and day, but somehow they made it work. When I was growing up, I always knew they genuinely loved and respected one another. Then my dad retired and everything changed. It was like their differences suddenly became insurmountable. I still don't get it," she said sadly. "I know they still love each other, but they can't seem to live together anymore."

"It happens." Cahill glanced out the window, his expression gloomy. "People change...grow apart."

"Is that what happened to you?" Pru hadn't meant to pry, but somehow the question just popped out before she had time to think how it might sound. "Did you and your wife...grow apart?"

If he was offended, he didn't let on. He studied the view for a moment before turning to face her. "Some people were never meant to be together."

The look on his face stunned her. It was as if, for one split second, she had been given a glimpse into all the pain, guilt and disappointment caused by the dissolution of his marriage, and she didn't quite know what to say. How to react.

"I'm sorry," she murmured. That he had shared something so personal, even inadvertently, left her at a loss. She wanted to say something to comfort him. Wanted to offer him a consoling hand, but that would be crossing a line into forbidden territory.

And Pru had a feeling that once that line was blurred, there would be no turning back. At least not for her.

A LITTLE WHILE LATER, Cahill walked Pru to her car even though she insisted it wasn't necessary.

"It's a nice night," he said as they headed down the steps of his building. "I could use some fresh air."

It was a nice night. By day, the temperature still hovered in the high eighties, but the evenings were noticeably cooler. And tonight there was a breeze blowing in from the south. Pru could almost smell the tang of salt from the Gulf.

As they walked across the parking lot to her car, she used the remote to unlock her door, but she didn't open it. Instead she turned to glance up at Cahill. "Can I ask you a question?"

He shrugged. "Shoot."

He seemed so tall tonight, Pru noticed. He was probably no more than five or six inches taller than her, so he certainly didn't hover over her. But he seemed to, so much so that she found herself catching her breath every time she gazed up at him.

"I saw you earlier in the bar," she said.

"That's not a question." Shoving his hands into his pockets, he leaned against the car. He seemed completely relaxed for a change, and Pru suspected few people ever saw him that way. It made her heart pound even harder.

"You were with Janet Stryker," she stated.

He shrugged again. "What of it?"

"Earlier, you were adamant that I not question her." Pru tried not to sound accusatory, but the shock of seeing them together still put an edge in her voice. "I can't help wondering—"

"If I'm hiding something?" he asked. "If I'm trying to protect her?" When Pru didn't answer, he said, "My meeting with Sgt. Stryker was strictly professional. And I happen to agree with you. Her relationship with Danny Costello is an angle worth pursuing."

"Then why did you tell me earlier to back off?"

"Because I've dealt with cops like Stryker before. You get on the wrong side of their egos, and they'll do everything they can to shut you out of the investigation."

"I...see." Pru paused, not as convinced as she wanted to be. "So did she tell you anything tonight? Anything useful about the case, I mean." Was she babbling? Pru couldn't really tell.

"She told me who hired Tripp's agency to investigate Clare McDonald."

Pru's brows shot up in surprise. "But Costello told me he had to sign a confidentiality agreement not to reveal the identity of the agency's clients."

"I never said Costello was the one who told her."

"Then who—"

"Max Tripp himself. It seems they have a bit of history, as well."

That didn't surprise Pru. A woman like Janet Stryker had probably left a string of broken relationships behind her on her climb to the top. Pru just hoped Cahill wasn't destined to become another of the woman's conquests.

"Please don't keep me in suspense," she said. "Who's the client?"

"Sid Zellman."

Pru gasped. She was surprised, and then again, she wasn't. She'd met the creepy little man, and nothing about him could shock her any more than his appearance had. "That fits, I guess. Clare even suspected him. Only, he wasn't the one who actually followed her, was he? It was his—"

"Surrogate."

The very word drew a deep shiver from Pru. She wrapped her arms around herself, suddenly chilled. "Zellman is one strange guy. He told me that he suffers from a condition similar to agoraphobia. He lives in the same building where he works, and he hasn't left the premises in over fifteen years. His assistant delivers everything he needs right to his door."

"Including the woman of his dreams," Cahill said.

"Oh, my God," Pru breathed. She was deeply disturbed by the visions suddenly playing out in her head. Sid Zellman...and Clare. "Have the police been able to connect him to Ellie Markham and Tina Kerr?"

Cahill shook his head. "No. And there's nothing tying him to Clare McDonald, other than the fact that he was having her followed by a licensed P.I. firm. Tripp Investigations may cross a few ethical lines, but they don't break any laws."

"Zellman knew about the posing of the bodies," Pru said. "He knew about the roses."

"Stiles could have told him once Zellman took on his case." Cahill paused. "Look, being weird isn't a crime. He may be guilty as hell for all we know, but as of right now, there isn't a shred of evidence linking him to any of these murders."

"So you think it's a dead end? A coincidence that he was having Clare followed?"

"I don't know about coincidence. I have a feeling they're all connected somehow...Stiles, Zellman, Tripp Investigations. I just can't figure out how. Sometimes I think..."

"What?"

"You said something the other day about the killer manipulating the MO, the crime scenes, even his own personality to throw us off track. What if we aren't dealing with a serial killer at all, Agent Dunlop? What if someone very clever wants us to think that we are?"

"Danny Costello implied the same thing tonight. He said we should go back to the basics. Look for means, motive and opportunity. Who has the most to gain from these women's deaths?"

"Maybe it's time we reevaluate," Cahill muttered.

"And in the meantime, another body could turn up." Pru bit her lip. "I don't think we're wrong about this. I think we are looking for a serial killer, a surrogate. Someone who kills to satisfy another's compulsions. Tiffany told me earlier about a club that she and Clare used to go to. A place called Acceleration on Montrose. She said she'd seen Janet Stryker there once. Maybe that's the reason Stryker was so forthcoming with information about Tripp Investigations. She knows that lead won't go anywhere because she's figured out who the killer is. Or at least, where and how he targets his victims. Maybe she's somehow trying to smoke him out on her own."

"That's a pretty wild leap, Agent Dunlop. Besides, in case you hadn't noticed, Janet Stryker hardly matches the killer's criteria."

"I realize it's a long shot," Pru said. "But I think we should check out that club. Show the victims' pictures around and see if anyone remembers them."

"Let's discuss it in the morning," he suggested. "We don't want to step on any HPD toes if we can help it. Right now, I think we should call it a night. We've both had a long day, and from here on out, they'll only get longer."

Pru nodded. "I'll get to the office as early as I can, but I'm meeting Tiffany at Clare's town house at ten to pack up some of her things." She started to open her car door, then turned back to Cahill. "Sir?"

His expression was inscrutable in the darkness. "What is it, Agent Dunlop?"

"I'm not exactly sure how to say this, but…" She decided to plunge right in. "I apologize for jumping to the wrong conclusions earlier. When I saw you in that bar with Janet Stryker after you'd told me to back off, I...well, I made some assumptions. I should have known better. You're too much of a professional to ever let personal feelings get in the way of an investigation."

He would never let personal feelings get in the way of an investigation, and neither should she. And yet at that moment, Pru had the wildest urge to kiss him until he had no choice but to respond.

She imagined the two of them in bed together, arms and legs entwined, bodies straining for release. She shivered at the image, but she pretended it was the breeze.

And he pretended not to notice. "I'm a professional, but I make mistakes just like everyone else," he said.

His voice deepened Pru's awareness. "I find that hard to believe. Not with your track record. You've broken some of the biggest cases in the country." She paused. "You are a legend, you know. Whether you believe it or not."

He straightened from the car and said gruffly, "You have to stop that, Agent Dunlop."

"Stop...what?"

"Looking at me that way. You and I both know it can't happen."

Pru almost gasped. She'd let down her guard for one split second, and he'd seen right through her. He *knew.* "What can't happen?" she tried to bluff.

"You know what I'm talking about." His tone remained stern, his expression implacable. "I saw it in your eyes just now. I felt it in the car yesterday when we were driving back from Huntsville. I'll admit, I'm attracted to you, too, but I repeat, it can't happen. It wouldn't do either of our careers any good."

He was attracted to her, too? Since when?

Oh, my God.

He was attracted to her, too! That was huge news. Wow news.

Pru fought the smile that tugged at her lips. The exhilaration that threatened to lift her right off the ground and into his arms.

"I…don't know what to say," she murmured.

"You don't have to say anything. I just wanted you to know where I stand."

"I, uh…okay. So…what do…?" She had no idea what she'd been about to ask him. Her mind was like mush. John Cahill was attracted to her. The impossible had happened, and Pru couldn't seem to form a coherent thought. She was almost grateful when he interrupted her, even if it was to smack her down again.

"We don't do anything about it," he said in that tight, harsh voice. Pru was beginning to find his gruffness very enticing. He was so wound up. What would it take to make him lose control? "We ignore whatever this is until it goes away."

"Okay, but…what if it doesn't go away?"

He frowned. "It will. It always does."

Maybe for you. But Pru's fascination with him had

lasted five years and counting. She was beginning to wonder if she would ever get over him. Maybe what she felt for John Cahill was something a little more than infatuation. Or even hero worship.

Of course, she couldn't tell *him* that. He was probably already second-guessing his decision to approve her transfer into SKURRT, and the last thing Pru wanted was to give him enough ammunition to boot her out. Her career still meant everything to her.

"I told you to stop that," he warned.

"What?"

He ran a hand through his hair. "When you look at me like that…"

"Like what?"

He gave a heavenward sigh. "I must be out of my mind. If someone had told me two days ago that I'd be standing here contemplating kissing you in my own parking lot…"

He wanted to kiss her?

Pru thought her knees would collapse right then and there. "Maybe you should stop contemplating it and just do it," she dared him.

"Didn't you hear any of what I just said?" he asked in exasperation.

"I heard every word," Pru said. "But I don't think it's going to go away." *It hasn't for me,* she wanted to tell him. *Not in five years.* "Maybe if we get it out of our systems…"

"Get it out of our systems," he muttered. "What

kind of cockeyed logic is that?" Almost against his will, he lifted his hand and ran his knuckles down the side of her face, wincing as if the feel of her skin was somehow painful to him. "What are we doing, Agent?"

"You were thinking about kissing me, sir."

Before he could change his mind, Pru moved in closer. "And I happen to think it's an excellent idea." She tilted her head so that he almost had no choice. "It's just a kiss, John."

But it wasn't. Not for her, and she suspected not for him, either. When his lips touched hers for the first time, it was one of those devastating moments that changed your life forever. Pru realized instantly that she was never going to be the same, and that knowledge frightened her even as she reveled in the feel of Cahill's mouth on hers.

Wrapping her arms around his neck, she pressed herself to him as his hands moved up and down her back. She hadn't kissed anyone in a very long time, and the sudden intimacy that sprang between them overwhelmed her. She was frightened, yes. Scared to death. But she didn't want the moment to end. Ever.

She tingled all over. Her scalp. Her breasts. Even her fingers and toes.

Pru was pressed so closely to Cahill that she could feel his body react, too, and it made her want him even more. It made her want to rip off all her clothes and make love to him right there on the hood of her car.

They broke apart, then he kissed her again, even more frantically the second time. Pru stood on tiptoes, kissing him back just as desperately. She could feel his heartbeat. It was a wild, hard rhythm that reminded her of voodoo drums, and she saw him in her mind, naked by firelight as he lowered himself over her.

His tongue was inside her mouth. Deep and demanding. She met him thrust for thrust, and when he groaned, the drumming inside her own chest exploded with urgency.

When they broke apart this time, they were both gasping for breath. Cahill was visibly shaken, but he didn't release her. Instead, he leaned against the car and pulled her to him. Gazing skyward, he said softly, "Houston, we have a problem."

She gave a tremulous laugh. "I can't feel my toes."

"Agent Dunlop—"

"My friends call me Pru."

His eyes glittered in the darkness. "We aren't friends."

They weren't lovers, either. Not yet…

"This can't go any further," he said with grim determination even has his arms tightened ever so slightly around her.

"I understand."

"Do you?" His voice lowered disapprovingly. "Then why are you still looking at me that way?"

"I can't help it," she said. "The way you kissed me just now…"

"It was just a kiss. You said so yourself."

"Right." But if it had been such an ordinary kiss, why couldn't she stop shaking? Pru wondered. Why couldn't he?

"I'm serious," he said. "This can't happen again, Agent."

"Yes, sir. Sir?" She drew a quick breath. "If it can't happen again, then maybe you should stop looking at *me* that way."

JESSIE COULDN'T STOP smiling as she let herself into her dorm room. Sarah was already in bed, so Jessie was careful not to wake her. Tiptoeing to the bathroom, she changed into her pajamas, brushed her teeth and washed her face, then glided silently to her bed and crawled underneath the covers.

Pulling the quilt up to her chin, she stared at the ceiling as she thought back over the evening.

It had been…magical. That was the only word she could think of to describe it. First, they'd gone to see a movie, and then afterward, they'd strolled around the darkened campus, talking for what seemed like hours.

Jessie could have stayed out all night with him, she found him so fascinating. He wasn't like anyone she'd ever known before, and she couldn't get over how well he understood her. It was as if he knew everything about her, although he couldn't possibly know about the rape. Her name had never been released to the public and she hadn't had to testify at her attacker's trial.

And yet he treated her as if he did know. It was as if he could somehow intuit her every need, her every fear.

That was because they were soul mates, he'd told her. And Jessie believed him.

He was never pushy or aggressive like some of the guys her age. He didn't even touch her when he kissed her, except for that butterfly brush of his lips. And Jessie was beginning to want more. Tonight, she'd even leaned into him, subtly inviting him to deepen the kiss, but he'd pulled away, whispering against her ear, "Patience."

"Patience," Jessie whispered to herself.

Growing drowsy, she rolled over and closed her eyes. It was the first time in a very long time that she went to sleep smiling.

Chapter Eleven

"John, for God's sake, do you have any idea what time it is?" Cahill's ex-wife demanded the next morning.

"It's almost nine," Cahill said absently as he rifled through a file. He'd already been at the office for hours.

"It's almost nine on a *Saturday morning,*" she grumbled. "You know I like to sleep in on my days off."

Cahill heard a man's voice in the background before she put her hand over the mouthpiece.

So the boyfriend had slept over. No wonder she needed her sleep.

Cahill waited for the inevitable pang of jealousy or a stab of resentment, but neither came. What he felt this morning was...strangely exhilarated.

He'd kissed Agent Dunlop the night before, and she'd kissed him back with the abandon and ardor of someone...well, someone ten years younger than him. The boost to his ego couldn't be overstated. Cahill didn't consider himself a vain man, but the way Pru had looked at him...the way she'd kissed him...

You are a legend, you know.

He wasn't a legend. Not by any stretch of the imagination. He was a man who'd probably just made one of the biggest mistakes of his career.

And yet he didn't regret that kiss. Instead, he found himself wondering when he might be able to kiss her again.

"John?" His ex-wife's voice jolted him back to the present.

"I'm still here."

"What's so all-fired important that you had to call me this early on a Saturday morning?"

"Have you heard from Jessie?"

"That's it?" she asked incredulously. "You're calling to see whether or not I've heard from our daughter? For God's sake, she's only a few minutes from your apartment, not halfway around the world. You could have called her yourself. Or gone by to see her." *Why bother me?* her tone implied.

"I've tried calling her for days," he said tightly. "She's been turning off her cell phone, and I never seem to catch her in the dorm."

"She's a freshman in college. She's busy being a normal eighteen-year-old girl. Don't take that away from her."

"I'm not trying to take anything away from her," he said defensively. "I just want to make sure she's okay."

"You have to stop this," Lauren scolded.

"Stop what? Caring about our daughter?" he demanded.

"You know that's not what I mean. You have to stop being so overprotective. You're smothering her. Why do you think she wanted to live in the dorm? She needs her independence, and you have to find a way to let her go."

"Let her go? She's my daughter," he said angrily.

"She's growing up. Daughters do that."

He ran a hand through his hair as he got up to pace his office. "I didn't call for a lecture. I just want to know if you've heard from her."

"She's fine. Leave her alone."

"Damn it, Lauren—"

"You can yell at me all you like, but we both know what this is about." She lowered her voice. "You still blame yourself for what happened to her."

Of course, he still blamed himself. If he'd been there that night—

"It wasn't your fault, John. It wasn't." Her voice caught, and he heard her draw a deep breath. "You'd give your life to protect her. We both know that."

Her words stunned him into silence. Since when had his ex-wife decided to be so generous?

"You weren't there that night and I didn't wake up," she said softly. "We both have to find a way to live with that. You're not to blame any more than I was."

"There was a time when you thought I was," he reminded her.

"I blamed you because it was easier than blaming myself," Lauren said simply. "My God, I was *there*.

I slept through the whole thing. Do you have any idea—" She broke off and sighed. "We can't go back and fix it. What's done is done. What we can do is move on. Make the most of our lives. We owe that much to our daughter."

"You've changed," he said, almost in awe. He could hardly get over it.

She laughed softly. "Yes, I guess I have. Maybe I've finally grown up, too. About time, wouldn't you say?"

Cahill could hear her puttering around in the kitchen as she made coffee. It was a homey sound that made him feel at loose ends.

"What's going on with you?" he asked suspiciously. "Why the big change? Is there something you want to tell me?"

She laughed again. "You always were perceptive. I guess that's why you're so good at what you do." She sounded very young suddenly, and it reminded Cahill of the way she'd been years ago, before the bitterness and resentment had made her so unhappy. She'd always felt stifled by their marriage, and she'd never missed an opportunity to let him know it.

"I'm getting married," she finally said.

Her announcement startled him, but he managed to recover. "Congratulations. When's the big day?"

"Not until next spring. I want Jessie to have time to get to know him. He's a great guy. I think you'd like him."

"You sound happy," Cahill said.

"I am. It's been a long time coming." Then realizing how her words sounded, she said quickly, "I didn't mean anything by that. It's just…well, I think we both know that we would never have stayed together for as long as we did if it hadn't been for Jessie. We were never suited for each other. I wasn't a good wife to you. I realize that now. I never supported you in your career. In fact, I probably made things worse because I never gave you a reason to come home."

"We both made mistakes," Cahill said.

"That's true. But I don't regret any of them because without them we wouldn't have Jessie. We did something right together. She's a beautiful girl, inside and out, and now she's growing up. She's growing away from us, and we have the opportunity to start our lives over. You're still a young man, John, and if anyone deserves to be happy, it's you."

He didn't know what to say to that. An emotion he didn't understand welled inside him. It had been a long time since he'd concentrated on anything other than his job and his daughter. And now he was losing them both. Jessie was growing up and he was leaving the Bureau. What in the world would he do with himself?

"I want you to find someone who truly deserves you," Lauren said. "Who truly appreciates the kind of man you are. But I don't think that can happen until you forgive yourself."

"You're asking a lot for a Saturday morning," he said gruffly.

She sighed. "I guess I am at that. Take care of yourself, John."

Cahill hung up the phone slowly, almost reluctant to let his past, as unhappy as it had been, drift away from him.

The future suddenly seemed just a little too scary and uncertain.

BY THE TIME Pru got to Clare's town house, it was a little after ten, but Tiffany was nowhere in sight. The property manager, a man named Grayson, had agreed to let them in, and as Pru wheeled into a parking spot in front of Clare's unit, she saw him check his watch.

She got out of the car and hurried across the parking lot toward him. "Mr. Grayson? I'm Agent Dunlop." She fished out her ID. "I'm meeting Tiffany Beaumont here this morning."

"Looks like she's a no-show," he groused. "I can't wait around much longer. I have an appointment in ten minutes."

"Maybe you should just go ahead and let me in," Pru suggested.

"Ordinarily, I wouldn't do that." He turned to unlock the door. "But if you can't trust the FBI, who can you trust, right?"

Pity more people didn't have that attitude, Pru

thought as she stepped inside Clare's town house. It would make her job a whole lot easier.

Grayson seemed reluctant to follow her in. He hovered on the threshold, his gaze darting about the interior. "Do you know what her family plans to do with this place?"

Pru shook her head. "Not a clue. I assume they'll eventually sell it."

"I don't mean to sound insensitive," he said, "but it's bad for the whole complex if a unit sits empty for too long. Especially one with such an unhappy history. People start to talk. Rumors swirl. Before you know it, buyers stop asking about the place. I suggest they unload it as soon as possible."

"I'm sure that's good advice, but I don't have anything to do with those kinds of decisions," Pru said.

He shrugged. "Thought you might like to pass it along." He glanced around again, and Pru thought she saw him shudder. "Are you sure you'll be okay here until your friend shows up?"

"I'll be fine. Don't worry about me."

"All right, then. Don't forget to lock the front door when you leave. I'll stop by anyway just to make sure."

"Thanks."

The moment the door closed between them, Pru felt an odd sense of disquiet settle over her. The town house still contained all of Clare's furniture and personal belongings, but somehow it had that strange, empty feeling that came with an abandoned property.

Slowly, Pru walked around the living room, trying to absorb the ambience of the place. If she closed her eyes, she could picture Clare at home that night, waiting for her would-be lover. She'd left work late so she must have been in a hurry when she stopped by the florist's shop and the liquor store. Then she'd come home to set the stage for what she'd thought would be a seduction.

Pru's gaze moved to the entrance as she imagined the scene that had unfolded that night.

Clare drew back the door and smiled. He had a single red rose in one hand, and he held it out to her. "For you."

She lifted the rose to her nose and inhaled the sweet fragrance. "It's beautiful."

"Just like you." He stepped inside the town house and smiled at her approvingly.

She whirled in front of him. "Do you like my new dress?"

"Yes," he said, his gaze darkening. "But I'll like taking it off of you even more."

Laughing, Clare lifted the rose again to her nose. "I thought of that, too, when I bought it. I've been thinking about it all day...."

He took her in his arms and kissed her, a deep, soulful kiss that made Clare tremble. "I want you," she whispered.

"Patience." He took her hand and led her into the living room. "Let's have some champagne, shall we? Be a shame to let it go to waste."

Pru moved over to the couch. The champagne bottle and crystal flutes had been taken to the lab for DNA analysis, but nothing had been found. The glasses had been washed and refilled with flat champagne before the killer left the premises that night. He'd taken great care not to leave anything of himself behind. He'd even washed his saliva off Clare's body.

While he popped the cork, Clare settled on the sofa beside him. When he handed her a glass, she said breathlessly, "What shall we drink to?"

"How about a night to remember?"

She clinked her glass to his. "A night to remember. I like that."

"Yes," he promised. "You will." He took the glass from her hand and kissed her again. "Put on some music. Something slow and sexy."

Pru moved over to the stereo and sorted through the CDs. The one that had been playing that night was still in the changer. Sade.

When the music started to play, Clare turned, surprised to find him right behind her. She hadn't heard him approach. He moved like a cat, she thought. Like a dark, sleek panther....

"Dance with me." He held out his arms, and Clare glided into them.

Winding her arms around his neck, she swayed against him.

"I like how you move," he murmured.

"I move even better in the dark," she said boldly. She stopped dancing and took his hand. "Let's go upstairs."

This time he didn't object. He followed her to the stairs and kissed her on the bottom step. He kissed her again on the landing and by the time they were in Clare's bedroom, she couldn't wait to have him.

The wilted rose petals led Pru up the stairs and down the hallway to Clare's bedroom. The images inside her head were so vivid that she almost expected to see Clare and her lover entwined on the bed.

"I want you," she whispered again. "I want you more desperately than I've ever wanted any man."

"And soon you'll have me." He unfastened her dress and slipped it off her shoulders. It slid to the floor in an elegant puddle, and then she removed her bra and panties. When she started to take off her stilettos, he said, "No, leave them on."

She smiled. "Whatever you say." She lay back on the bed, completely uninhibited. He stood at the foot, staring down at her. "Aren't you going to join me?"

"Of course. But first I have a little present for you."

"A present?" She lifted herself on her elbows, her lids heavy with desire. "What is it?"

"You'll see." He removed something from his jacket pocket and then, climbing onto the bed, he straddled her, lifting her hands high above her head.

"What are you doing?" Clare asked in alarm when she felt the leather straps cut into her wrists.

"Don't fight it," he whispered. *"Just relax and enjoy it."*

"But—"

He kissed away her doubts, and when he finished securing her wrists to the bedposts, he kissed his way down to her ankles.

She trembled as he moved back over her.

"Close your eyes, Clare."

She did as he asked, still not sensing the danger until he slipped the leather strap around her throat. And then it was too late....

A sound downstairs jerked Pru out of her reverie and, thinking that it was Tiffany, she hurried outside to the landing. "Tiffany? Is that you? I'm upstairs."

No answer.

"Tiffany?" Pru started down the stairs. As she neared the bottom, the hair on the back of her neck lifted, and she knew, even without the curious sound, that she was no longer alone.

She drew her weapon as she silently descended the remaining steps. The front door stood slightly ajar. Grayson had closed it earlier, which meant that someone had come in after he left.

Her grip tightening on her gun, Pru walked slowly around the room. She checked the entry-hall closet, the tiny home office off the living room, and finally, she moved toward the kitchen door and pushed. She met with resistance at first, and then the door swung back on her. Pru had to jump out of the way to keep from being hit.

Danny Costello stood in the doorway, gazing at her in a way that made her blood run cold. She had only a brief glimpse of his dark eyes before the door swung closed between them again.

But in that instant, Pru had seen something else, something that made her heart pound with fear. Someone had been in the room with Costello. A darkly clothed figure hovering in the background.

Pru barely had time to digest what that meant before the door swung open, and Costello lunged forward. He staggered literally into her arms, and the weight and force of his body sent them both crashing backward. Pru's head hit on the bottom stair as her gun went flying.

Her skull exploded in pain, and for a moment, she lay in a daze, the weight of Costello's body knocking the breath from her lungs.

She knew he was dead even before she saw the knife in his back. Panic welled inside her and she gasped for air as she tried to scramble out from under him.

Her gun lay just beyond her grasp, and as Pru struggled to reach it, a gloved hand closed over it.

Danny Costello's killer was dressed all in black, his face hidden behind a dark ski mask. But Pru could see his eyes. They were dark and gleaming. Completely without remorse.

Stepping over her, he held the gun in both hands as he aimed for her head. For one terrible moment, Pru could do nothing but stare up at him.

I know you, she thought. *I know what you've done.*

Then the front door opened and Tiffany called out, "Pru? Sorry I'm late—"

The killer's head whipped up, and Pru used that split second of distraction to kick at his legs. He'd thought she was pinned by Costello's body, and her assault must have caught him completely by surprise.

He lost his footing and went sprawling to the floor. The gun sailed out of his hand and spun across the slick hardwood.

From the doorway, Tiffany screamed.

Pru and the killer lunged for the gun. Her hand closed around it first, and she rolled, firing.

The killer dove through the kitchen door.

Pru's first instinct was to pursue him, but as she rose to her feet, the room started to spin and her knees buckled.

Chapter Twelve

Cops swarmed Clare's town house. Two uniformed officers had arrived first, followed by Janet Stryker and Barry Reed. Then a man who introduced himself as Lieutenant Mayberry came in, and while they all huddled over Danny Costello's body, Pru sat on the sofa with an ice pack pressed to her head and Tiffany, verging on hysteria, clinging to her hand.

Pru wasn't exactly the picture of calm, either. She didn't want to think about what might have happened if Tiffany hadn't shown up at the town house when she had. Without the distraction, the killer would have shot her point-blank.

Shivering, she clutched the ice pack to her head. She had no idea how long she'd been sitting there when, through the aching throb, she became aware of a new voice in the room. A familiar voice. A voice that made her heart pound, but not in fear.

She spun to face Cahill and the sudden action sent

a sharp pain shooting through her skull. She leaned back against the sofa and tried to stifle a groan.

Spotting her from the doorway, Cahill strode over and sat down beside her. "What happened?"

"He got away," she said wearily. "The killer was here. He was here in this very room. I saw him. I could have taken him out—"

"You could have been killed yourself," he said.

Her pulse quickened at the note in his voice. At the way he looked at her. "I'm okay."

"Are you sure about that? You don't look so good." He turned to one of the cops. "Where are the paramedics?"

"They're on their way, sir."

"I don't need the paramedics," Pru said. "I need to get back to work."

"Come on," he said, taking her hand.

"What are you doing?"

"I'm taking you to the E.R. Head injuries are nothing to fool around with."

Janet Stryker overheard and came scurrying toward them. "I wouldn't recommend that. It's not standard procedure, and besides, we need a statement from Agent Dunlop."

"You'll get your statement," Cahill said in a tough, grim voice. "Right now, I have an agent who needs medical attention. I don't give a damn about your procedure."

Stryker looked as if she wanted to object again, but

one glance at Cahill's face and she swallowed whatever protest was on her tongue. She gave Pru a cold, hard once-over, and Pru thought the woman's eyes were every bit as menacing as the killer's.

WHAT THE HELL was taking so long? Cahill wondered as he paced the E.R. waiting room. They'd taken Pru back forty-five minutes ago, but no one had seen fit to tell him what was going on, even when he waved his badge under their noises.

So much for being a legend.

He could only conclude that the head injury was more serious than they'd originally thought. If she had a concussion, the doctor would probably order a CAT scan and an MRI, and that could take hours.

He had just started to approach the nurses' station again when he saw Charlie Dunlop rush through the glass doors of the E.R. A petite woman hurried after him, and Cahill knew immediately that she was Pru's mother. She was blond, slender and gorgeous. Dressed to the nines, she did look a little like Grace Kelly.

"Where's Pru?" Charlie demanded.

"She's still in with the doctor," Cahill told them. "They won't let me go back because I'm not next of kin."

"I'd like to see them try and stop me," the woman said ferociously. She left her ex-husband's side and stormed up to the nurses' desk where she conversed for several long minutes before returning to the two men.

"She's in Room 103. One of us can go back with her."

"You go on," Charlie said. "I'd like to have a word with Agent Cahill."

At the mention of his name, the woman glanced up at him curiously. "I know your name," she said. "Have we met before?"

"I don't think so." Cahill was pretty sure he would have remembered her. Like her daughter, she was not a woman who would be easy to forget.

She patted her ex-husband's arm. "I'll tell Pru you're here."

He nodded absently.

After she glided away, Charlie put a hand on Cahill's shoulder. It wasn't a friendly gesture. "Let's take a walk."

They ended up in the hospital cafeteria, two cups of lukewarm coffee on the table in front of them.

"So what happened?" Charlie's tone was cool, assessing.

Cahill filled him in as best he could. When he was finished, the older man's eyes turned dark. "My daughter could have been killed. That's what you're telling me."

"But she wasn't," Cahill said. "Her training and instincts kicked in and she handled herself like any good agent would. You should be proud of her."

"You don't have to tell me how to feel about my daughter. She means everything to me, Cahill."

"Believe me, I understand."

"I know you do," Charlie said. "And that's why I'm going to talk to you here, father-to-father."

Cahill frowned. "What is it?"

"Whatever is going on between you and my daughter needs to stop right now."

"I don't—"

Charlie gave him a sage look. "I wasn't born yesterday, Cahill, and neither were you. I saw something on your face when you were in the waiting room just now, and I see that same something in Pru's eyes every time she mentions your name. You two are headed for trouble."

"You've obviously read the situation wrong," Cahill said. "There's nothing going on between Pru and me."

"It's Pru now, is it?" Charlie leaned across the table, his expression sober and, even in his sixties, still menacing. "She has a hell of a lot more to lose here than you do, Cahill."

"I realize that." Good Lord, he thought. He was nearly forty years old. How had he gotten himself in the uncomfortable position of being chastised by a woman's father?

"You do anything to hurt her or her career and you'll answer to me. Is that clear?"

Cahill's own gaze never wavered. "I have no intention of hurting Agent Dunlop. Personally or professionally."

Charlie didn't look all that convinced, but he shrugged. "I figure I'm probably whistling in the wind, but I wanted you to know how I feel. Pru's special. I hope you realize that."

"I do," Cahill said. And he meant it.

PRU WAS SITTING on the edge of the bed waiting for the doctor to give his okay for her to leave when the door burst open and her mother sailed in.

"Mom! What are you doing here?"

"My only daughter was very nearly killed today. Where else would I be but at her side?" She rushed over and wrapped her arms around Pru. "Honey, are you okay? When I heard what happened—"

"I'm fine. But how did you know I was here?"

"Tiffany called. She's beside herself, Pru. First Clare and now you…" Her mother's arms tightened around her.

Pru relaxed against her mother for a moment, and then she drew away. "I'm fine, Mom. Really. The doctor says it's nothing serious. Just a bump on the head."

"Are you sure that's all it is?"

"Positive. I'm getting out of here as soon as he signs the paperwork."

"That soon? I don't know if that's such a good idea. Head injuries can be extremely tricky, Pru. I'd like to speak to the doctor myself."

"Don't you dare talk him into keeping me here,"

Pru warned. "I assured him that if I had any headaches or dizzy spells, I'd come right back."

"I'm at least going to drive you home and look after you," her mother insisted.

"I appreciate the offer, Mom, but I'm going back to work."

"Don't be ridiculous, you'll do no such thing. Your dad and I are driving you home, and I don't want to hear another word about it."

Pru stared at her mother. "Dad's here, too? With you?"

She looked a bit sheepish. "I called him as soon as I heard from Tiffany."

"And you two came together?"

Her chin lifted. "I was too upset to drive."

"I see. And just where is Dad now?"

"He's talking to Agent Cahill."

"What about?" Pru asked in alarm.

Her mother gave her a cagey look. "Maybe you should tell me."

"I don't know what you're talking about."

"Not much you don't." Her mother sighed. "Oh, Pru, I saw the way you looked just now when I mentioned Agent Cahill's name. You're in love with that man."

Pru's mouth dropped. "*In love?* Mom, come on. He's a colleague. We work together. That's all there is to it."

"All there is to it? I don't think so," her mother said

slowly. "I know who he is, Pru. I've seen his name in the paper. I've heard your father talk about him. I've heard *you* talk about him."

"He's a good agent," Pru said lamely, wishing her mother wasn't quite so observant. Pru would never hear the end of it now. Not until she confessed everything.

But the trouble was, she wasn't sure what to confess. She'd thought her feelings for Cahill were nothing more than a misplaced crush, but after they'd kissed last night, she'd done some serious soul-searching. What she felt for John Cahill wasn't an inconsequential infatuation. She wasn't just attracted to him. She cared about him. Deeply. And although she might not yet be in love with him, Pru had a feeling that she was well on her way.

Question was, did he feel the same way?

Her mother gave her a disapproving look. "He may be good at what he does, but that man comes with a lot of baggage, Prudence."

"Don't we all?" Pru muttered.

"He's divorced, with a grown daughter."

"You're divorced, with a grown daughter," Pru snapped. "Does that mean you aren't entitled to be happy?"

"You know what I mean."

"Mom, there's nothing going on between Agent Cahill and me, so stop worrying, okay?"

"Your mouth says one thing, but your eyes tell a very different story," her mother accused. "You're a grown woman so you can make your own decisions, but I just wish…"

"What? What do you wish?" Pru said wearily.

"I wish I didn't have the feeling that you're about to get in over your head," her mother fretted.

A LITTLE WHILE LATER, Cahill stood at the window in his office staring out at the traffic. But when he heard Pru approach, he turned, his gaze shadowed with something she couldn't quite name.

"What are you doing here?" he said grumpily. "I thought I told you to go home."

"I'm not going home," she said. "We've just had our first major break in the case, and I'm not about to sit on the sidelines because I've got a bump on my head."

"The doctor told you to take it easy," he reminded her.

She shrugged. "If you were in my place, would you go home?"

"You do have a hard head. I'll give you that."

"Lucky for me that I do," she said with a grin. She was still shaken by the morning's events, but she didn't want Cahill to see how unnerved she really was.

"Pru…"

She caught her breath at the way he said her name.

"I think we need to talk about what happened at my apartment last night."

"Nothing happened. Not really. We kissed. That was it." Pru bit her lip. "If you're going to tell me that it can't happen again, don't bother. I heard you last night. Sir," she added softly.

"Stop calling me sir."

His sudden anger took her aback. "What should I call you then?"

"I don't know." He let out a long breath as he gazed down at her. "I'll be honest with you. I don't know what to do about this."

"You said if we ignored it, it would go away."

"And you said if I kissed you, it would get it out of my system. So why is it that I want to kiss you again, Agent? Why is it, that's all I seem to be able to think about?" He closed his eyes briefly. "This is crazy. I'm too old to be acting this way."

"It's okay," she murmured. "It's all I can think about, too."

His gaze darkened. "Then we've got a problem. You see that, don't you?"

"Yes, I suppose I do."

He turned back to the window. "Do you remember what I told you the other day? This job takes incredible dedication."

"I remember you said it's the first thing you think about when you wake up in the morning and the last thing on your mind before you go to sleep. And then you dream about it," Pru said.

He nodded. "There's a reason for that. You have to be focused. But more than that, you have to be consumed by your cases. You have to live and breathe them. You have to be willing to crawl inside a killer's mind and stay there until you understand what makes him tick. You can't do this job with distractions. It has to take priority over everything else. No matter what's going on in your private life, you have to be willing to shut out everything and everyone else. Do you understand what I'm saying?"

"Yes, I understand," she said in resignation.

"Do you still want this job, Agent Dunlop?"

She answered without hesitation. "More than ever."

"Then you have to make a choice. It's as simple as that."

She knew what he was saying and she knew he was right. But that didn't stop her heart from sinking. "What if I can't make that choice?" she whispered.

"You have to. I can't make it for you. It has to happen in here." He lifted his hand and touched her temple, then slowly stroked his knuckles down her cheek. The tenderness in his gesture made her tremble.

Their gazes locked, and for a moment, Pru thought he would kiss her again. He couldn't help himself because the attraction between them was electric. An irresistible pull that weakened resolve and made common sense fly out the window.

She felt it, too.

Her eyes fluttered closed in anticipation, and then a noise from the doorway interrupted them. Cahill's hand dropped from her cheek.

Across the room, Tim Sessions cleared his throat.

"Uh, sorry to interrupt, I just heard about Danny Costello."

His gaze moved to Pru, whose face suddenly flamed. They'd nearly been caught kissing, and that was exactly the sort of thing Cahill had been warning her about. They'd been so distracted neither of them had heard Tim come in.

She glanced up at Cahill, and knew that he was thinking the same thing. His jaw hardened.

He turned away with a scowl.

Tim's gaze moved back to Pru. "Are you all right?"

"Just a bump on the head," she assured him.

"Did you see who attacked you?"

She shook her head. "He wore a ski mask. I only saw his eyes."

"What about a physical description?" Tim pressed.

"He was dressed in black and he was thin."

"Are you sure it was a man?"

Pru lifted a brow. "What?"

The younger agent shrugged. "If he wore a mask, how can you be so sure the assailant was male?"

"He was tall," Pru said.

"Tall for a man or tall for a woman?"

She cocked her head. "What are you getting at, Tim?"

"Nothing. I'm just trying to jog your memory, that's all. It's obvious that this changes things."

"What do you mean?"

"For one thing, it eliminates one of our suspects."

"He's right. This changes everything." Cahill spun and strode over to his desk and sat down. He was careful not to make eye contact with Pru. "The killer let you see him. He's either getting careless or desperate."

"Which is why he took out Costello." Tim plopped down in the chair next to Pru's. "He knew Costello had seen him, too."

"How do you know that?" Pru asked. She hadn't yet had a chance to relate her conversation with Costello to Tim.

He shrugged. "Stands to reason. Costello had Clare under surveillance. He must have seen the killer at some point." He paused. "And now you've seen him, too."

A chill slithered up Pru's spine, but she tried to ignore it.

"So what's our next move?" Tim asked Cahill.

Cahill's gaze finally met Pru's and in those dark depths she saw something that might have been a challenge. "Agent Dunlop? Any ideas?" *Or are you still too distracted to think clearly?*

Her own gaze was unwavering. She made sure of it. "In the Atlanta child-murder cases, the police and the FBI decided to go proactive when all their leads dried up. They devised a media strategy to lure the killer out, and it worked. He was apprehended within days. Maybe that's what we need to do. Find a way to draw the killer out."

"A proactive campaign is not without risks," Cahill warned. "It can backfire. Embolden the killer or cause him to go underground."

"I realize that," Pru said. "But I'm not suggesting we do the same thing the police did in Atlanta. We know that our guy goes after young, blond professional women who live alone. What if we give him a target?"

"Whoa," Tim said. "I'm with Agent Cahill. That sounds extremely risky, especially for the target."

"Not only risky, but damn near impossible to pull off," Cahill said. "A sting operation like that could take weeks to put in place. And you'd have to find a female cop or FBI agent willing to set herself up as bait."

"I could do it," Pru said.

Cahill shrugged, his expression still neutral. "You don't match the criteria. Besides, you're forgetting that the killer already knows who you are."

"I could change my hair, alter my makeup, my wardrobe. I look completely different as a blonde," she said. "*You* wouldn't even know me with my natural hair color."

"I wouldn't count on that," he muttered.

"We could start with the nightclub that Tiffany told me about," Pru insisted. "The one she and Clare went to. I make an appearance there for the next few nights and if no one takes the bait, then we broaden our net until we get him. We set up a pen pal relationship with Stiles. We hire Tripp Investigations to follow our target. We do whatever it takes to draw this guy out into the open."

Tim gave her a skeptical look. "What happens if he does take the bait?"

Pru's hands were still trembling. She didn't dare look at Cahill. "We get him before he gets me."

Chapter Thirteen

Cahill wasn't the only one who had noticed her. A number of heads turned when she walked into the club, and from his discreet table, he watched her make her first pass through the crowd.

Across the room, Cahill caught Tim Sessions's eye, and the younger agent nodded almost imperceptibly. He'd seen her, too.

They had been staking out Acceleration for nearly a week, and Cahill wondered, not for the first time, if they were wasting their time. If the killer was cruising the club for his victims, he had yet to show his hand.

Their time might better have been spent establishing a pen pal correspondence with John Allen Stiles, but against his better judgment, Cahill had allowed Agent Dunlop to convince him to put the club under surveillance. He trusted her instincts, but at the same time, he hoped they weren't making a terrible mistake, one that could blow up in their faces if they weren't careful.

The club gave off some disturbing vibes. The atmosphere was dark, smoky and seductive...the perfect backdrop for the young women who came looking for thrills. They wore short skirts and high heels, and the men wore the same predatory gleam in their eyes. Cahill figured most of them were harmless, but one guy in particular had caught his attention.

The man had come into the club every night that Cahill had been there, and the way he stared at the women sent a chill of apprehension down Cahill's spine. He sat alone in the corner, his dark gaze coldly assessing as he ordered drink after drink that sat untouched before him.

Cahill watched him watching the blonde, and he frowned. He didn't like any of this. Something about the whole setup worried him.

His gaze darted about the club, but his attention always came back to the blonde. Her routine never varied. Night after night she came alone to the club and would pause just inside the door to scan the room before finding a table. But she rarely sat alone or for long. She liked to dance, and Cahill liked to watch her.

The man in the corner watched her, too.

Ignoring the leers and sidelong glances, she walked with steady purpose toward the back of the club, and as she passed Cahill's table, their gazes collided.

A jolt of electricity shot through him. He still couldn't get used to how different Agent Dunlop looked as a blonde. She'd been right. He never would have known her.

The way she dressed didn't hurt, either. She chose stylish but sexy outfits, usually in black, that showed a lot of leg and the barest hint of cleavage. She had a killer body. Why hadn't he noticed those curves before?

After a few moments, she took to the dance floor, moving with abandon as she lifted her hands over her head and pumped her body in time to the music.

Now and then, she would glance at him and Cahill's heart would race in spite of himself. But mostly she danced with her eyes closed.

He almost felt like a voyeur, Cahill realized. As if he were watching her in her most intimate moments.

The man in the corner seemed to think so, too. He stared at her through dark, hooded eyes, then abruptly he got up and walked out of the club.

Cahill made eye contact with Pru, nodded, then rose and followed the man out.

Cahill trailed the man out to the parking lot. "Hey, buddy, you forgot your wallet!"

The man turned, and when he saw Cahill striding toward him, waving a wallet, he hesitated. He felt in his jacket pocket, then seemed to visibly relax. "It's not mine."

He started to turn away, but by this time, Cahill had caught up with him. "You sure?"

"Look, pal, you've got the wrong guy, okay? My wallet is right here." He pulled it out of his pocket and held it up.

"Must be a mix up then. The waitress said you left

this wallet on the table. Maybe you'd better check just to make sure."

The man's gaze narrowed. "What is your problem? *This* is my wallet. *Comprende?* Now back off."

"I'm afraid I can't do that." Cahill flipped open his wallet. "I'm a federal agent. I'd like to ask you a few questions."

The man's gaze dropped to Cahill's badge and ID, then lifted. Something that might have been fear glimmered in his eyes. "What does the FBI want with me?"

Cahill reached over and snatched the man's wallet. "May I?" Before he could protest, Cahill flipped it open and scrutinized his credentials. The man's name was Gerald McBride. He had a Texas driver's license, two credit cards and a Texas Association of Licensed Investigators membership card.

Cahill glanced up. "You're a P.I.?"

"I'm licensed," he said defensively. "And I have a permit to carry a concealed weapon. If you've got a beef, it's not with me. I'm legit."

"Who do you work for?" Cahill asked.

"Tripp Investigations."

Cahill's voice sharpened. "You're here working a case." It was a statement, not a question.

The man nodded. "Surveillance. Look, I apologize if I've stepped on your toes. I'm just trying to do a job."

"Who's your subject?" When he didn't answer,

Cahill said, "You're in a pretty dicey situation here, Mr. McBride. It seems you've inadvertently stumbled into a federal investigation. I can't necessarily make you cooperate, but you and I both know it would be better for you if you did."

McBride hesitated, then shrugged. "I'm tailing a woman. A blonde. I have a picture of her here somewhere."

When he reached inside his pocket, Cahill tensed.

Slowly, McBride withdrew his hand. "Easy," he said. "I'm just getting the woman's picture." He held it out to Cahill.

The photo had been snapped as Pru came out of the club that first night. Cahill recognized the dress she'd worn and the impact it had had on him when he'd first spotted her in it.

Someone had hired Tripp Investigations to investigate Pru.

Someone who saw her as the woman of his dreams?

The killer?

"Do you know her name?"

"Not yet. But I'll find out soon enough," McBride said. "Unless..."

Cahill lifted a brow. "Unless what?"

"Unless she's the reason you're here. That's it, isn't it? I'm not the only one who has her under surveillance. The feds are interested in her, too. What'd she do?"

"You ask too many questions, McBride." Cahill slipped the picture into his pocket. "Now I've got a question for you. Who hired you?"

"I don't know."

Cahill took a menacing step toward him. "Like I said, it would be better for you if you cooperate."

"I don't know," the man said again. "All I know is that I was told to come down here and keep an eye on her. If you want more information than that, you'll have to talk to Max Tripp. But I doubt he'll tell you anything without a court order."

"We'll just have to see about that."

"Are we done?" McBride demanded.

"For now," Cahill said. "I'll be in touch, though."

McBride looked as if he wanted to say something else, then thought better of it. He turned and high-tailed it across the parking lot. Cahill watched him until he heard someone call out his name. Turning, he saw Tim Sessions hurrying toward him.

"What's going on?" the younger agent asked breathlessly. "You find out who he is?"

"Gerald McBride. He's a P.I. with Tripp Investigations."

Tim's mouth dropped. "You're kidding."

"I wish I were," Cahill said grimly. Things were moving a lot faster than he'd anticipated. The truth of the matter was, he'd discounted Tripp Investigations all along, even when Pru had insisted the agency was a viable lead. Cahill had been so sure that Stiles was behind the murders, but McBride's appearance had thrown him for a loop.

"You think the killer hired Tripp Investigations to follow Pru?" Tim asked worriedly.

"I don't know. It seems a little too coincidental that a perfect stranger would notice her and have her investigated. But there's something about this whole setup that bothers me," Cahill mused. "I can't help thinking…"

"What?"

"The killer has been manipulating us all along. And he's still manipulating us."

"So what are you going to do?" Tim asked.

Cahill drew a breath. "I'm taking Pru off the case."

Tim looked startled. "You can't do that! This whole thing was her idea. And it's working. The killer is taking the bait—"

"He's not taking the bait," Cahill said angrily. "Don't you get it? He's orchestrating this whole thing."

Tim frowned. "How?"

"I don't know," Cahill admitted. "But somehow he's been ahead of us every step of the way. We've played right into his hands, and now Pru's life is in danger."

"You can't take her off the case," Tim said. "It'll kill her career."

"Right now I'm a little more concerned about keeping her alive." Cahill pulled out pen and paper from his pocket and started scribbling. "Get back to the office and see what you can find out about McBride." He handed Tim the piece of paper. "Here's his license plate number. Let me know what you find out."

Tim took the paper and stuck it in his pocket, but he made no move to leave.

Cahill scowled at him. "What are you waiting for?"

"This situation with Pru…"

"If you've got something to say, spit it out," Cahill snapped.

"I can't help wondering if you're letting your personal feelings for her affect your judgment…sir. That's not like you and, frankly, it worries me."

"Your concerns are duly noted," Cahill said coolly. "Now get back to the office and find out what you can about McBride."

PRU SAW Cahill at the door, and at his nod, she followed him out. When she emerged onto the street, she glanced around. He was nowhere in sight.

She turned to go back inside the club, but a hand caught her arm. She whirled, her heart in her throat, but it was Cahill. He drew her away from the door and into the shadows.

Before she had time to catch her breath, he pressed her up against the wall and kissed her.

His kiss had been devastating before, but now he seemed to be staking his claim. He touched her in ways that made her gasp for breath.

Pru wrapped her arms around his neck and pressed herself against him. "What's going on?" she whispered against his lips.

He hesitated. "I'll explain later. Let's just get out of here."

"But…" She broke off as she realized they weren't alone.

Someone was watching them.

The man in the shadows never moved. His gaze remained fastened on Pru.

And then she recognized him. It was Greg Oldman, Sid Zellman's assistant.

A woman came out of the shadows then, laughing and stumbling as she clung to his arm. Another blonde, Pru noticed, and as the woman and Oldman walked past where Pru and Cahill still stood, she saw the woman's face.

Her resemblance to Clare was astonishing.

Chapter Fourteen

When Pru's doorbell rang later that night, she knew who it was without looking through the peephole. She drew back the door, and Cahill silently brushed past her.

"We have to talk."

"I know."

She'd changed out of the black dress into a robe and had scrubbed all the makeup off her face. Only the blond hair remained of the woman Cahill had kissed earlier. Pru wondered if she would still have the same effect on him.

"We've let this thing get out of hand," he said. "It never should have gone this far."

He paced back and forth in her living room, as if he couldn't quite bring himself to look at her. "I won't compromise the integrity of my unit because we can't control ourselves."

Pru frowned. "But nothing happened."

"Not yet." He stopped pacing and glanced at her. "You and I both know it's just a matter of time. After tonight…we can't kid ourselves. The way you looked…the way you danced…I couldn't keep my hands off you." As if to demonstrate, he walked over and placed his hands on her arms. "I should have put a stop to this right from the start. But I didn't and now…"

"And now what?" she asked almost fearfully.

"One of us has to leave SKURRT."

Pru could not have felt more stunned if he'd physically attacked her. "You can't mean that."

"I mean every word of it." His grip tightened on her arms. "Please understand something. If I could be the one to leave, I would. But I can't. You're not ready yet, and I can't leave the unit shorthanded. I'm sorry, but it has to be you."

Pru stared up at him. "John, don't do this."

"It's done," he said grimly. "I've already talked to Glen McCurry at Quantico. He has an opening on his team. I gave you my highest recommendation. He wants you there first thing on Monday morning."

Pru gasped. "Just like that? Without consulting me?"

"It's the only way. The Bureau can't lose you, Pru. You're too valuable. By the time you're ready to head up a unit yourself, I'll be gone. You can come back here then, if you still want to, and if we still feel the same way about each other…" His eyes softened as he stared down at her. "Who knows?"

"So that's it then. I'm out." Pru felt like crying but she wouldn't give him the satisfaction.

"You're not out. Glen McCurry can do far more for your career in Washington than I ever could down here. You have a big future ahead of you, Pru. I'm not going to be the one to take that away from you. I couldn't live with myself."

His hands slipped from her arms, but Pru wouldn't let him go. "You've made an awful lot of decisions for me tonight. And there's not a damn thing I can do about any of them. So I'll go back to Quantico and I'll work for Glen McCurry. I'll do what I've always intended to do. But there's one decision you can't make for me."

"And that is?"

She took his hand and drew him toward her bedroom.

SLOWLY, SHE UNFASTENED her robe and let it slip from her shoulders. The moment Cahill realized she wore nothing underneath, his gaze deepened. He said nothing at first, but his eyes told Pru everything she wanted to know. He wanted her, as much as she wanted him.

His hand snaked out to cup the back of her neck and roughly pull her to him. He kissed her so hard, Pru thought she would shatter into a million pieces. He groaned against her mouth as his hands found her breasts, the sensitive skin between her thighs.

When she could stand it no longer, he lifted her and

she wrapped her legs around him, kissing him over and over as they stumbled down the hallway to her bedroom.

She lay back on the bed and watched him undress. She'd seen his body before, but not all of him. The sight of him made her tremble. Made her reach out for him...

"Please tell me you brought protection," she whispered as he moved over her.

He reached down and took something out of his pocket.

Grabbing the package from him, she ripped apart the foil, rolled the condom onto him and then guided him to her.

He froze and closed his eyes briefly. "It's been a while. I don't know..." He plunged inside her then, and Pru gasped at the sensation. Arching her back, she lifted her hips to meet his.

It was over almost before it began. For both of them. Pru couldn't hold back. She wasn't a virgin, but it was as if she'd been saving some part of herself for Cahill all these years. And now that the moment was at hand, she gave herself with abandon.

Her body began to tremble uncontrollably as she clutched at his back. He held her so tightly she could hardly breathe, and a moment later, he shuddered to his own climax.

He collapsed on top of her and groaned. "That was...way too fast," he muttered.

"Speak for yourself."

"Pru…"

"Don't. Don't you dare say it was a mistake."

"I wasn't going to. I was just going to say that…I can do much better."

"I might die if you were any better," she said with a sigh. "John…"

He rolled off her and pulled her against him. "What?"

"Are you going to miss me?"

His arms tightened around her. "You have no idea."

She turned and studied his face. "Don't find someone else while I'm gone, okay? Give us a chance."

"There is no one else like you," he said simply. "I didn't think I could ever feel this way again." He gave a short laugh. "I don't think I ever have felt this way."

"I know I haven't. I've wanted you since you walked into that classroom at the academy five years ago. The great John Cahill…" She put a hand to her mouth. "I can't believe I just slept with you."

"Hardly a legendary performance," he muttered with regret. "I told you once before that I don't belong on your pedestal."

"Yes, you do. You have no idea how great you really are," she said softly. "I think that's why I love you so much."

SHE LOVED HIM? *My God,* Cahill thought. What had he done?

He was sending her away, and if she came back to

him, even in six months, she wouldn't be the same woman. Not after working in SKURRT.

The job would change her in ways she couldn't imagine, and even as he held her in his arms and watched her sleep, he could feel her slipping away from him.

His cell phone rang, and her eyes flew open. "It's mine," he said softly as he eased himself out of bed. "Go back to sleep."

Picking up his jacket, he fished his cell phone from his pocket and lifted it to his ear. "Cahill."

"John? Oh, God…I'm so glad I caught you…"

"Lauren?" He cradled the phone against his shoulder as he automatically began to get dressed. "What's wrong? You sound upset?"

"It's Jessie…"

Cahill's heart jumped. "What about her? Is she okay?"

"That's just it. I don't know where she is. I've been trying to reach her all day. I know I lectured you about this very thing, but…I have a bad feeling something is wrong. I don't know what to do—"

CAHILL WAS DRESSED and out of her apartment before Pru had time to catch her breath. One look at his face when he hung up the phone, and she'd known instantly that something was wrong.

"John, what is it?"

He turned to her, his gaze haunted. "That was my

ex-wife… She hasn't been able to get in touch with Jessie. Her roommate hasn't talked to her since early this morning, and no one else has seen her, either. Lauren's afraid…she's gone missing."

"Missing?" Pru put a hand to her throat. "Oh, my God. You don't think…"

"That her disappearance has something to do with this case?" He closed his eyes briefly. "I don't know. Dear God, if anything happens to her—"

Pru placed her hand on his arm. "Don't think the worst. She's eighteen years old. There could be any number of explanations."

"I know. I keep telling myself that, but the truth is, I've had a bad feeling something wasn't right with her for days. I should have gone to see her. I should have pried it out of her. If anything happens to her after everything else, I'll never be able to forgive myself."

The guilt would kill him, Pru thought. He'd never be able to get over it.

Aloud she said, "What can I do?"

"Stay by the phone." He finished dressing and strode toward the door. "I may need you to assemble a team on a moment's notice."

"I'll be ready. John?"

He paused at the door and glanced back.

"We'll find her, okay? We will."

But Pru could tell from his expression that her encouragement had failed to convince him.

Seconds after she heard the front door close, she

climbed out of bed and headed for the shower. She carried the phone into the bathroom with her so that if it rang, she would be able to hear it over the running water.

She showered and dressed as quickly as she could, and just as she reached for the phone to carry it back into the bedroom with her, it rang.

Snatching it up, she pressed the call button. "John?"

"No, it's Tim. I was hoping he was with you. I've got some news."

"About Jessie?" Pru asked anxiously.

"Jessie? Who's Jessie?"

"I just thought—"

He cut her off. "No, this is about Tripp Investigations and the P.I. they sent to the club tonight."

Pru frowned. "P.I.? What are you talking about, Tim?"

"Agent Cahill didn't tell you?"

"Tell me what?"

There was a long silence. Pru could picture Tim running a hand through his hair. "I shouldn't have called your number."

"Well, you did call it," Pru said impatiently. "Now tell me what's going on. Tripp Investigations sent one of their investigators to the club tonight? And John…Agent Cahill knew about it?"

"I can't believe he didn't tell you himself," Tim muttered.

"You said you'd found out something. What is it?" Pru prodded.

Tim paused. "I don't want to get into it over the phone. I'd like to see you and Agent Cahill in person."

"Agent Cahill was called away on another case," she said. "But I can meet you at the office."

"No, wait. I'm about five minutes from your place. I'll drive over."

"All right," Pru said. "I'll be waiting."

A few minutes later, she drew back the door and motioned for Tim to enter. He brushed past her and hesitated, his gaze darting about the apartment.

"You're alone?"

"I told you. Agent Cahill was called away on another case. Have a seat," Pru said, as she moved to the couch. Tim sat down beside her. "Tell me about this investigator."

Tim still seemed hesitant. "His name is Gerald McBride."

"What was he doing at the club?"

"Watching you."

Pru gasped. "Watching me? How do you know that?"

"Because that's what he told Agent Cahill. He even showed Cahill a picture of you that had been taken a few days earlier as you left the club. My guess is, he's had you under surveillance since you first started going to Acceleration."

Pru tried to suppress a chill at the notion of someone—the killer, perhaps—watching her. "Do you know who hired him?"

"No, not yet. But get this. He's only been working for Tripp Investigations for a few months. Before that, he worked exclusively for Linney, Gardner and Braddock. And since we know that Sid Zellman hired Tripp's agency to tail Clare, I'd say that gives us reason enough to lean on Zellman."

An image of Sid Zellman materialized in Pru's head, and she tried to suppress a shudder. Was he their man? She had no way of knowing. Not yet. But the evidence was starting to mount up.

And now he—or someone—had obviously targeted Pru. That had been her intent…to use herself as bait to draw out the killer. And the plan appeared to be working.

Why hadn't Cahill told her about the P.I.? Why hadn't he warned her that she might very well be in the killer's crosshairs?

Because *his* plan was to get her out of the way. Her sudden transfer to Quantico made a lot more sense to Pru now. Cahill was trying to protect her.

She wanted to be flattered that he cared enough about her safety to go to such extremes, but at the moment, all she felt was betrayed.

He didn't trust her. He didn't have faith in her abilities as an agent. She could take care of herself, but obviously, Cahill didn't agree.

Beside her, Tim said, "I think we should get over

to the Texas National Bank Building and confront Zellman before he has a chance to cover his tracks."

Pru shook her head. "You can't make a move like that without authorization."

Tim gave her a strange look. "Don't you mean 'we'?"

Pru ran a hand through her hair. "I'm off the case, Tim. I'm out of SKURRT."

His mouth dropped in astonishment. "Since when?"

"A little while ago. I'm being transferred. I'm expected back at Quantico first thing Monday morning."

Tim stared at her, speechless. Then abruptly he turned away. "This changes everything."

"Yeah, I know. It sucks. But there's not much I can do about it. I really don't want to go, especially until I find out about Jessie."

"Jessie." Tim turned with a frown. "Cahill's daughter?"

"She's gone missing. John's worried that her disappearance could have something to do with this case."

"You mean…he thinks the killer has Jessie."

"Right now, he's putting all his energies into finding her, and rightfully so."

"I'm sure she's okay," Tim murmured. "Maybe a little seasick…"

Pru caught her breath. "What do you mean by that?"

Tim sighed. "Your leaving really does change everything. Unfortunately, it's a little too late to help me."

Pru was beginning to get a very bad feeling about this conversation. "Tim...what are you talking about?"

"I wasn't good enough for SKURRT," he said. "Cahill kept turning down my transfer requests. 'Not psychologically compatible for the job,' he said. 'Doesn't have the right instincts.' As it turns out, I'm a little more clever than he gave me credit for. I've had HPD running in circles for months. And now Cahill." He gave a bitter laugh. "He's like a puppet on a string. He goes exactly where I want him to go."

Pru's purse was lying on the chair next to the couch. Her gun was inside. If she could reach it—

As if intuiting her intention, Tim whipped out his own weapon. "Don't even think about it. We've got a long night ahead of us, Pru. Might as well relax."

"You killed those women because your transfer was refused? Why?"

"To prove a point. I warned you on that tape. I'm not like any killer you've ever known before. I kill for one reason and one reason only. Because I can."

The phone rang on the couch between them, and—weapon still on her—Tim snatched it up. "Hello, Agent Cahill," he said into the mouthpiece.

Pru tense as she watched him, waiting for that moment, that one split second, when he might let down his guard.

"Here's the deal," Tim said, his gaze still on Pru. "You told me once that agents who are accepted into SKURRT have to make tough choices all the time.

You told me that turning down my request for a transfer—*three separate times*—was one of the toughest choices you'd ever had to make. But you were wrong. That didn't even come close. Because now you have to decide between your daughter and your girlfriend. Even the great John Cahill can't save them both."

He hung up the phone and tossed it back on the sofa. "Get up," he said to Pru.

She rose slowly. "Where are we going?"

"You'll find out soon enough." He motioned with his gun toward the door. "Get going. Nice and slow. I don't want to have to shoot you here, but I will. You know what I'm capable of, don't you?"

His voice sent a chill up Pru's spine. She turned. "Just tell me one thing. Why Clare? Because she knew me?"

"That was just a happy coincidence," he said.

"And the other two victims?"

"The victims don't matter," he said with a careless wave of his hand. "They could have been anybody as long as they had the same physical characteristics as Stiles's victims."

"Because you wanted HPD to think they had a copycat killer on their hands."

"Or a surrogate. You and Cahill were only too eager to play along. Then you stumbled across the information about Danny Costello, and once I realized he may have seen me, I had to get rid of him. But that only added a new dimension to the game, didn't it?

Tripp Investigations, Sid Zellman, John Allen Stiles…
like I said, I had you and Cahill running in circles."

"All right, you're clever," Pru said. "I'll give you
that. But why Jessie? She's just a kid."

"Because I want him to know what it feels like to
lose everything. It's as simple as that."

Out of the corner of her eye, Pru saw her purse in
the chair. Tim couldn't see it from where he stood. She
kept talking to him, trying to draw his attention. The
phone rang again on the couch, and when he turned
she grabbed the gun, turned and fired.

The bullet hit him in the arm and he screamed. Pru
dove behind the chair, and kept firing.

Tim screamed again as another bullet connected
and then he fell back through the window.

Pru heard his body thud against the ground as she
bolted from her cover and rushed to the door. By the
time she got outside, he was gone.

PRU HAD THE PHONE to her ear as she sped down the
I-45 Corridor toward Galveston. When Cahill finally
picked up, she said breathlessly, "I know where she is."

"Pru? Oh, my God, are you okay?"

"I'm fine, but Tim got away. I wounded him, but I
don't think it was serious enough to stop him. He
said that Jessie was okay except for maybe being seasick. Tim has a boat. He keeps it in Galveston. He and
my father used to go out fishing sometimes. It's called
The Mermaid's Lair. It's docked at the Galveston

Yacht Club. I'm on my way there now, but I don't know if he's in front of me or behind me."

"I'm still in Champions," Cahill said. "You've got at least a twenty-minute head start on me. Pru, wait for backup, do you hear me? I'm calling the Galveston PD right now."

"All right, but tell them to hurry," Pru said as she hung up the phone.

CAHILL LIFTED the phone to his ear. "Cahill."

"You've probably heard from Pru by now," Tim Sessions said tightly. "She thinks she's figured out where your daughter is, but here's the deal, Cahill. I'm not in this alone. I have someone watching Jessie at this very moment, and if my partner so much as hears a police siren, your daughter is fish bait. You understand?"

"You're bluffing," Cahill said.

"Am I? Are you willing to take that chance with your daughter's life? I don't think so."

The phone went dead in Cahill's ear.

Swearing violently, he called Pru. She picked up on the first ring. "I just talked to Sessions."

He heard her catch her breath. "What did he say?"

"He says he has someone watching Jessie. If I call the police, they'll kill her."

Pru said nothing for a moment. "Do you think he's bluffing?"

"I don't know. He's been one step ahead of us so

far. I think we have to assume he's planned for every contingency."

"I agree."

"So here's what I want you to do. Pull over. Let me handle this. I'm the one he wants."

"I can't do that," Pru said. "Besides, I'm almost there. I may be ahead of him. I could get Jessie off that boat before he ever shows up."

"And if he does have someone watching the boat, you could be shot before you ever get on board," Cahill said grimly. "I can't let you take that chance."

"He's not going to kill me," Pru said softly. "Not until you get there. He wants you to have to make a choice. Your daughter…or me."

Cahill's jaw hardened. "Pru…"

"Don't," she said softly. "Don't say anything. You and I both know that if it comes down to it, there's no choice to be made here."

JESSIE HAD TRIED every way she could think of to get off the boat, but the hatches were locked from the outside. She was trapped.

What if no one came for her?

Jessie trembled with fear and revulsion as she thought about what might happen when he came back. She tried frantically to open the hatch again, but then she stopped and listened as the boat rocked at its moorings.

Someone had come on board.

She could hear waves lapping against the hull, and every so often the houseboat swayed as someone moved about the deck. Then she heard footsteps outside, and she placed her ear close to the door.

"Jessie?"

It was a woman's voice. Jessie rapped on the door. "I'm in here. I can't get out."

The locked rattled. "Stand back, honey. I'll get you out of there."

She huddled against the wall as the door came crashing in. Jessie didn't know the woman, but she thought she'd never seen anyone so beautiful. Without hesitation, she collapsed in the woman's arms.

"IT'S OKAY," Pru said. She wrapped her arms tightly around the shivering girl. "I'm going to get you off this boat, but we have to hurry." If she'd had time to get here, Tim would have, too. They had to hurry.

She took Jessie's hand. "Come on, honey."

They slipped as quickly as they could along the darkened deck, and Pru scrambled up to the dock, then bent to offer Jessie a hand.

"I can't let you do that, Pru. I can't let you take her."

Pru whirled. Tim slowly came toward her in the darkness. One hand clutched his wounded arm, the other gripped his weapon. "This is almost too perfect," he said. "I can take care of you both in one fell swoop. Then we'll see how clever Cahill thinks I am."

"Drop the weapon!" Cahill called from the darkness.

Tim didn't flinch. "I'm going to take one of them with me, Cahill. It's your choice."

"Let them go. You don't want to do this."

"You're wrong," Tim said. "I'm going to enjoy breaking you. The great John Cahill…" He lifted his weapon, but before he could get off a shot, John fired.

Tim squeezed the trigger, but the shot went wild. And then the gun fell from his limp fingers as he tumbled back into the water.

Jessie scrambled to the dock and started running. Cahill met her halfway, and swept her up in his arms. "I'm here, baby," he whispered over and over as his daughter sobbed in his arms.

His gaze met Pru's in the darkness, and she could see that he was crying, too.

He reached out to take Pru's hand, and she lifted it to her lips.

Epilogue

One year later…

The sun was setting over the Gulf as Pru descended
the steps to the pier. She'd checked the office of Sea
Quest Charters and found it empty so she figured Cahill would be out on the dock admiring the company's
latest acquisition, a thirty-foot Sportfisherman chris-
tened *The Dreamcatcher.*

Jessie was on board along with her first mate, Kyle
Newcastle, a smitten A&M marine biology student,
as they prepared for the boat's maiden voyage. When
Jessie saw Pru, she lifted her hand and waved.

"You're just in time!" she called.

Pru waved back. "Thanks, but I think I'll sit this
one out!"

At the sound of Pru's voice, Cahill turned and gave
her a lazy smile. "You'll miss a great sunset."

"Funny, I don't feel like I'm missing anything,"
she murmured as she walked over to stand beside him.

He draped an arm across her shoulders. "So how was work?"

She drew a long breath and released it.

"Don't feel like talking about it?" he asked.

She shook her head. "No, not yet. I just want to stand here and enjoy the scenery."

"I understand."

And Pru knew that he did. That was one of the things that made coming home to him so wonderful. She didn't have to talk about her work. She didn't have to apologize for the mood shifts or the brooding silences. For the cases that consumed her, changed her. She didn't have to explain anything because Cahill had been there.

The Dreamcatcher lifted anchor, and with one final wave, Jessie expertly steered the fishing boat toward the open sea.

"She looks happy," Pru murmured.

"I think she is."

"That boy is in love with her, you know."

Cahill winced. "I was trying not to notice."

"Has Jessie?"

"Be kind of hard not to, wouldn't it? The way he's always hanging around."

Pru gave him an admonishing look. "He's a good kid, John. Be nice."

"I know. He is a good kid. And I think he's good for Jessie."

Pru's brows soared. "Wow. That's quite a concession, coming from you."

"About time, wouldn't you say? But a lot's changed. *I've* changed." Cahill pulled her closer. "If you'd told me a year ago that my daughter and I would be running a business together, I never would have believed it. Much less a charter fishing company," he said dryly. "But it was a good decision. For both of us."

"For all three of us." Pru wrapped her arm around Cahill's waist. "If you'd told me a year ago that I would be married to the great John Cahill, I never would have believed it. But here we are."

"Here we are," he agreed. "Which reminds me. Your mother called earlier. You have a fitting for your maid of honor dress tomorrow at ten."

"*Matron* of honor," Pru corrected him. A tiny thrill shot up her spine. "Can you believe it? My parents are actually getting married. I was beginning to think that it wouldn't happen again. They're both so stubborn. But I guess true love wins out every time."

"I guess it does."

"Just look at us. When you sent me back to Washington last year, I wasn't sure I'd ever see you again. Or if I would ever be able to forgive you. But then you showed up on my doorstep and asked me to marry you…"

"And you said yes."

"Was there ever any doubt about that?" she asked ruefully. "I've wanted you from the first moment I laid eyes on you. I wanted you when you didn't even know I was alive."

"Hard to believe there ever was such a time." His eyes turned dark with emotion. "Because now I can't imagine my life without you." He bent and kissed her. "I love you."

"I love you, too."

His arm came around her again as she leaned her head against his shoulder and together they watched the sun slip lower and lower, until all that remained was a glimmer of light on the horizon.

That bit of light, Pru thought, was all she would ever need to guide her home from the darkness.

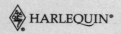

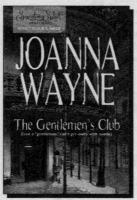

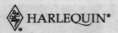